SCARLET SAILS

by *Alexander Green*

translated from the Russian by Thomas P. Whitney

illustration by Esta Nesbitt

Charles Scribner's Sons   New York

F
G

SCARLET SAILS

A NOTE ON ALEXANDER GREEN

Alexander Green is one of the most popular of all Russian writers in his native land. In 1965, his collected works appeared in the Soviet Union in a six-volume, hard-cover edition of which 463,000 sets were sold. In recent years repeated printings of from 100,000 to 300,000 copies of his most popular stories have sold out almost as soon as they were published. There are never enough copies available to meet the great demand for his works.

Green is adored by Russian readers. In Leningrad there is a fan club in existence whose young members call themselves "The Scarlet Sails." They wear special insignia, and devote themselves to the study of Green's works and the furtherance of his literary heritage.

From his writings one does not recognize Alexander Green as a Russian. His pen name sounds un-Russian. His works, including SCAR-LET SAILS, are set in a mythical "Western" land where places have such un-Russian names as Caperna, Lisse, and Zurbagan, and people are called Asole, Grey, Longren, and Thomas Harvey.

The appeal of Green's writing is universal. It lies very much in the exotic, romantic, faraway atmosphere that he creates. Because of this he has been compared to Edgar Allen Poe, Robert Louis Stevenson, and Bret Harte. Yet Alexander Green was as Russian as samovars. He was born Alexander Grinyevsky, in 1880, in the Russian backwoods town of Vyatka and lived his entire life in Russia. The only foreign country he ever visited was Egypt, where he went on shore leave for a few hours in Alexandria from a ship on which he was employed. Green aspired to travel throughout the world, but he was never able to do so. He hoped to sail the seven seas, but in this, too, he failed, except in the richness of his imagination. Until his late twenties he was a failure in everything. He tried to become a sailor but did not make the grade. He prospected for gold in the Urals and found none. He worked in the rough and tough oil town of Baku as a roustabout and nearly died of the hardships he suffered. He enlisted in the Russian army and deserted. He became a member of the anti-Tsarist revolutionary underground and was arrested, jailed, then exiled.

It was after these experiences that he began to write, and as a writer he was immediately successful. From 1906 on, he began to be widely published in Russia. When the Revolution came in 1917, he had already acquired a considerable reputation. Yet, despite his fame, he nearly died of illness and hunger in 1921, after having served in the Red Army. It was in this period that he wrote SCARLET SAILS. A model boat that he saw in the window of a toy store in Petrograd (later Leningrad) in 1917 or early 1918 inspired the book. He carried his manuscript with him while in the army and completed it during a slow convalescence from typhus. SCARLET SAILS was published in part in 1922 and in its complete version in 1923. It became a Russian classic, beloved not only by the young but by readers of all ages. It formed the basis for a beautiful ballet created in the late thirties and was made into a motion picture in 1961.

After completing SCARLET SAILS, Alexander Green went on to write many more books. In 1923 he moved to the Crimea, where he died of cancer at the young age of fifty-two. His short stories, novels, and tales of adventure are known to nearly all Russian readers, but none of his books is quite as popular or as beautiful as SCARLET SAILS.

Alexander Green experienced at first hand all the suffering and all the poverty that were to be found in Russia, for his life was hard from beginning to end. But out of his imagination he wove rich and vivid stories filled with sunlight, gaiety, and adventure, stories that have brought joy to millions of people.

Thomas P. Whitney

Longren had been sailing as a seaman on the tight three-hundred-ton brig, *The Orion,* for ten years. He'd become more attached to her than many a son to his mother. Then he had been forced to give up the sea.

Here is how it happened. He had returned from a cruise—such visits home were infrequent. When he had walked to within sight of his small house in the fishing village of Caperna, he expected as always, when still a good distance away, to see his wife Mary on the threshold, waving to him, and as he came closer, running breathlessly to meet him. But this time she wasn't there. Instead, when he reached his cottage, he found an excited woman, their neighbor, standing beside a child's crib which had not been there before.

"Look at your daughter, my friend!" said the woman. "I've been taking care of her for the past three months."

Longren grew pale. He bent down to look at the tiny creature not yet eight months old, who was staring fixedly at his long beard. Then he sat down, cast his eyes to the floor, and began fingering his mustache, still wet from the rain.

"When did Mary die?" he asked.

The woman told her story, interrupting herself to murmur tenderly to the baby and to assert again and again that Mary was in paradise. Longren, once he had learned the details, could only feel that such a paradise was as dank and dark as the inside of a woodshed, that for the woman who had departed into that unknown country, true paradise would have been merely to sit beneath the light of a lamp with her baby daughter and her husband, returned from the sea.

Three months before Longren came home, the young mother had run out of money. She had been forced to spend more than half the amount he had left her on doctor's bills for herself and for the newborn baby after her difficult delivery. Unfortunately she had also lost the remainder, which, though not a large sum, was all

6

she had to live on. She had tried to borrow money from the local innkeeper and shop-keeper, Manners, who was known to be well-to-do.

Mary had been to see him at six in the evening. The neighbor had met her at seven on the road to the nearby town of Lisse. Tearful and desperate, Mary had told her that she was going to town to pawn her wedding ring. Manners had agreed to a loan, but only in return for her love.

"We've not a crumb to eat in the house. I must pawn my ring so that the baby and I can somehow get along till my husband comes home."

It was cold and windy out. The neighbor had tried in vain to persuade the young woman not to walk to Lisse after dark.

"You'll be soaked through to the skin, Mary! It's drizzling already, and with this wind, there's bound to be a downpour soon."

From the seaside village to the town and back was a good three hours walk, but Mary refused to listen to the woman's advice.

"I've been enough trouble as it is," she said.

"There is hardly a family to which I don't owe bread or tea or flour. I must go. That's all there is to it."

She walked to town, returned, and the next day came down with a fever. Exposure to the bad weather and the night rain had resulted in pneumonia in both lungs, according to the doctor called to her bedside by their good neighbor. A week later Mary's bed was empty, and the woman had moved in to take care of the baby girl. She was a widow and alone, and it had posed no great problem for her.

"Anyway," she added, "I'd be bored stiff without the little one."

Longren went off to town, collected his pay, said farewell to his comrades, and returned home to bring up his little Asole, as he had named her. As long as the baby could not walk by herself, the widow continued to live at the sailor's home acting as foster mother. But as soon as Asole learned not to fall when she stepped across the threshold, Longren announced that he himself would look after her. He thanked the woman for her help and sympathy and took up the lonely life of a widower, centering all his plans, hopes, love, and memories on his child.

Ten years of wanderings hadn't left him any the richer. He set to work. Soon his little toys began to appear in the stores in town. They were beautifully made models of rowboats and sailboats, speedboats, one-masted and two-masted schooners, cruisers, and steamers. In short, he made what he knew about at first hand. And what he made replaced for him, at least in part, the bustle of seaports and the picturesque life of the sea, and he earned enough to live a modest, frugal life. He had always been taciturn. After his wife's death he became even more unsocial and reserved. True, on holidays he sometimes could be seen at the local tavern. But he never sat down. Standing at the bar, he quickly gulped down his drink and took his departure, muttering brusquely to the right and left, "Yes," "No," "Hello," "Good-bye," or "Just a little," in reply to the greetings and queries of his neighbors. He couldn't stand entertaining guests. When people came to see him, he cut their visits short with such broad hints that they themselves soon thought up some excuse to leave. He never called on anyone. It was not surprising that an air of estrangement soon separated him from his fellow-villagers. If in his work Longren had been more dependent on local people, he would quickly have been made to feel the consequences of such bad relations. But he had almost nothing to do with the village. He bought all his food and goods in town. Manners had never sold him so much as a box of matches. Longren even did his own housework and patiently taught himself the complexities of the unmasculine art of raising a daughter.

Asole was five. Her father had begun to smile ever more softly when he looked at her nervous, yet gentle, little face as she sat on his knees and worked at unbuttoning his vest, or sang wild and rollicking sailors' chanties. The songs, delivered in her childish voice which sometimes missed the letter "R," had about the same effect as a dancing bear wearing a light-blue ribbon.

It was at this time that an incident took place,

the shadow of which fell on Longren and also darkened the childhood of Asole.

It was early spring and just as cruel and severe as winter though in a different way. For three weeks a sharp offshore north wind had been pressing against the cold earth.

The long row of keels of the fishing boats, which were pulled, bottoms up, onto the beach, looked, silhouetted against the sand, like the fins of an enormous fish. No one was foolhardy enough to go out fishing in such weather. One hardly saw a single person on the one and only street of the hamlet. The icy blast driving out from the hillocks of the shore to the empty horizon made the open air a torture. All the chimneys of Caperna worked from morning to evening, tumbling their smoke down the steep rooftops.

But these days of the north wind drew Longren from his warm cottage more often than did the sun and the sheets of airy gold it cast over the sea and Caperna whenever it came out in clear weather.

Longren would go out on a wharf built along

rows of pilings. He would stand for hours at the end of the plank pier, smoking his pipe, fanned by the wind, watching the sea floor, laid bare at the shoreline, grow smoky with gray foam on the heels of the waves. The water's thundering course to the black and stormy horizon filled the whole expanse with herds of fantastic, maned creatures driving in wild, uncontrolled despair to some distant consolation. The groans and moans, the roaring cannonades of enormous torrents, and the almost visible rush of wind which bathed the entire scene in its current had a deadening, deafening effect which helped dull Longren's grief. His tortured face relaxed as if in the troubled sadness of a deep sleep.

On one such day, twelve-year-old Hin, Manners' son, discovered his father's boat being beaten against the pilings beneath the pier and ran to tell him. The storm had only just begun. Manners had forgotten to pull the boat up on the beach. He went down to the water. Longren was standing at the end of the pier smoking, his back to him. No one else was out. Manners hurried to the middle of the pier, let himself down toward the churning water, got into the boat, and untied the moorings. He remained standing, and since he had no oars, began to pull the boat to shore by grasping one piling after the other. He stumbled momentarily and missed a pile. At that instant a strong gust of wind caught the prow of the boat, tearing it away from the pier toward the open sea. Stretching out as far as he could, Manners now could no longer reach the nearest piling. The wind and the waves rocked and drove the boat out into the water's fatal expanse. Realizing the danger, Manners was about to jump into the water to swim to shore, but he was too late. The boat was already turning and twisting beyond the end of the pier where the might and fury of the waves promised certain death. The distance between Longren and Manners, who was being carried out into the stormy deep, was no more than seventy feet. Not an impossible distance, since right under Longren's hand on the pier hung a coil of rope with a weight at its end—rope usually thrown from the pier to help boats dock in stormy weather.

"Longren!" screamed the terrified Manners. "Why are you standing there like a lump? I'm being carried away! Throw me the rope!"

Longren was silent. He watched Manners in the boat bobbing up and down. His pipe burned brightly, and taking his time, he removed it from his mouth to get a better view of what was happening.

"Longren!" Manners cried. "You hear me! I'm perishing! Save me!"

Longren said nothing. It was as if he had not heard the desperate call at all. He did not even shift from one foot to another until the boat had been carried out so far that Manners could hardly be heard. Manners screamed in terror. He begged the sailor to run for help. He promised him money. He threatened and cursed, but Longren only edged a bit closer to the tip of the pier to keep the struggling boat in sight as long as possible.

"Longren!" he heard dimly, as if listening indoors to the muffled shouting of someone on the roof. "Save me!"

At that moment, drawing in his breath deeply

so that not a word would be lost in the wind, Longren shouted: "That's what she asked you to do! Think about that while you're still alive, Manners, and don't forget it."

The cries faded away and Longren went home. Asole, when she awoke, saw her father in deep thought, sitting before the guttering lamp. At the sound of his daughter's voice he went over to her, kissed her fervently, and pulled her blanket up over her shoulders.

"Sleep, darling," he said. "The morning's still far away."

"What are you doing?"

"I've spoiled a toy, Asole. Go back to sleep."

The next day the missing Manners was the only topic of conversation in Caperna. After five days he was brought home, dying and furious. The story he told quickly flew through Caperna and the surrounding villages. Manners had been carried out to sea till nightfall. He was beaten against the side and bottom of the boat as it struggled through the wild waves which ceaselessly threatened to toss the crazed shopkeeper into the sea. He was that same night picked up by the steamer *Lucretia* on its way to Cassette. Influenza and shock killed Manners. He lived only forty-eight hours after his return, during which time he called down on Longren all the misfortunes and catastrophes that he could think of. Moaning and breathing with difficulty, the dying man told how Longren had watched him being carried out to sea and had not lifted a finger. Longren's deed naturally astounded the people of Caperna. For one thing, few among them had ever experienced so terrible a hurt as Longren had suffered or could grieve so intensely as he grieved for Mary to the very last day of his life. But what was most repulsive, incomprehensible, and utterly astonishing to them was that Longren had kept his silence. He had not uttered a sound until those last shouted words. He had stood there watching, unmoving, severe and calm, like a judge. He had shown his profound contempt for Manners. In his silence there had been so much more than mere hate. And not a person failed to sense this. If he had only screamed, expressed his joy at Manners' plight in gestures, or shown pride in his own maliciousness, the fishermen might have understood. But he had acted differently from the way any of them would have acted. His conduct was utterly incomprehensible. He had set himself above everyone else, and by so doing had committed the unforgivable.

From then on no one nodded to him, reached out to shake his hand, or even cast a glance of recognition or greeting in his direction. Once and for all he was excluded from the affairs of the village. Little boys when they saw him would cry. "Longren drowned Manners!" He paid no attention. It was as if he didn't even notice that in the tavern or on shore, among their boats, the fishermen kept silence in his presence, avoiding him as if he had the plague. The Manners affair completed his estrangement from the village. Once total, it created a mutual hatred whose shadow fell on little Asole.

The small girl grew up without friends among the village children. There were only two or three dozen children near her age in Caperna.

Like sponges, they soaked up the prejudices of their parents. Little Asole was soon placed beyond the pale of their interest. It did not happen all at once, but came about gradually, as a result of repeated scoldings and prohibitions. Finally there developed an awesome taboo, which gossip and malice magnified in the minds of the children into a dreadful fear of the sailor's cottage.

Longren's now totally secluded way of life helped to feed the tongues of gossip. It was rumored that the sailor had murdered someone somewhere, and that was why he no longer went to sea. Longren, they said, was gloomy and antisocial because he was "torn by the pangs of a guilty conscience." When Asole came near the village children at play, they chased her away, or threw mud at her, and taunted her by calling her father a "cannibal" and a "counterfeiter." Her efforts to make friends with the other children all ended in bitter tears, in black and blue marks, scratches, and other manifestations of "public opinion." In the end she ceased to take offense, but now and then she would ask her father: "Why don't they love us?"

"Oh, Asole," her father would say, "do you think that people like that can really love? One has to be able to love, and that's beyond them."

"What do you mean—be able to love?"

"Like this!" And he would take the little girl into his arms and tenderly kiss her sad eyes, which squinted in satisfaction.

Asole's favorite amusement were the stories her father told her. Evenings or on holidays when her father had put away his glue cans, his tools, and his incompleted toys, had taken off his apron and seated himself, relaxing with pipe in mouth, she would climb up on his lap. And there, encircled by his arms, she would point to the different parts of the toys he was making and ask what they were for. In this way there began Longren's fantastic talks to his daughter on life and people—talks in which Longren's former way of life, accident, luck, and fortune, surprising and unusual events, played a principal role. Longren, as he taught Asole the names of ropes and rigging, of sails and ship's tackle, would become inspired by his subject. The uses of windlass, wheel, or mast, the type of ship they were discussing, would remind him of some incident or anecdote. From them he would branch out into seafaring adventures in which superstition was interwoven with reality and reality with his own fantasy. In these stories he told her of the "tiger cat" who was the herald of a shipwreck; the flying fish who talked and whom one heeded or else went off course; of the Flying Dutchman and his violent crew; and of omens and ghosts, mermaids and pirates; all the fables and fairy stories with which sailors whiled away the time when their ships were becalmed or as they sat in their favorite taverns. Longren told also of shipwrecks and their victims, of people who had grown wild and forgotten how to speak, of hidden treasures, of the mutinies of galley slaves, and much more. The little girl listened to all of this perhaps even more attentively than those people who first heard about Christopher Columbus' discovery of a new continent.

"Tell me more, please," Asole would beg when Longren fell silent. She would fall asleep right there on his breast, full of wonderful dreams.

For a more practical reason, it also made her very happy when the storekeeper came from town, eager for Longren's toys. So as to flatter her father and get his price down, he always brought some apples, a bit of pastry, and a fistful of walnuts for the little girl. Longren hated to bargain and usually asked only the going price for his work, but the buyer tried to get the toys even cheaper.

"Look here," Longren would say, "I've worked a whole week over this ship's launch." The model was nearly ten inches long. "Just look at its strength, its draft, its quality. It's a boat that will carry fifteen men in any kind of weather." And then it all ended with the quiet humming of the little girl over her apple. The sound undermined Longren's determination, and he accepted the buyer's price. The shopkeeper, after filling his basket with beautiful,

high-quality toys which he had bought at a bargain price, departed, laughing up his sleeve.

Longren did all his own housework. He split
the wood, carried the water, fired the stove. He
did the cooking and the laundry and the ironing.
Besides all this he managed to earn money.
When Asole was eight years old, her father
taught her to read and write and now and then
began to take her to town. Finally he sent her
by herself, when there was need to collect
money for toys that had been sold or to de-
liver new ones. This did not happen often,
though Lisse was only a few miles from Caperna. The road led through the woods and
there was much there that could frighten a
child. True, it was not so much physical danger that was to be feared so close to a town,
but even that was possible. Therefore it was
only on lovely mornings when the roadside
was bathed in a sea of sunlight, calm, and
flowers, at a time when Asole was least likely
to be threatened by the phantoms of her lively
imagination, that Longren let her make the trip
alone.

Once, about halfway to town, the little girl sat down beside the roadway to eat a piece of meat pie placed in her basket for lunch. While she ate, she examined the toys. Two or three were new to her. Longren had made them at night while she was asleep. One of the new pieces was a miniature racing sloop. The white craft bore scarlet sails made from pieces of silk which Longren ordinarily used only for finishing the insides of cabins in steamers in the toys for rich customers. But, having made the sloop, he had found no suitable material for the sails and had simply used what he had, pieces of the scarlet silk. The sloop delighted Asole. The blazing, jolly color burned in her hands as brightly as a flame.

The road at this point was intersected by a stream crossed by a narrow log bridge. "What if I put it in the water to sail a bit?" thought Asole to herself. "After all it won't get wet through and I can wipe it off."

Following the woods downstream a way, beyond the bridge, the little girl placed the sloop which so enthralled her into the water. The gleaming scarlet of the sails was immediately reflected in the transparent water. The sunlight shining through the fabric cast a trembling rosy light on the white stones of the river bed.

"Where do you hail from, Captain?" Asole asked in a commanding voice, and then replied for him:

"I've come . . . I've come from China."

"And what have you brought?"

"That I won't tell you."

"So that's the kind of captain you are! I'll put you right back in the basket."

The captain was about to reply submissively that he had only been joking and was prepared to speak when a light but sudden offshore breeze turned the prow of the sloop toward the center of the stream. And like a real sloop taking off from shore, it floated at full speed down the current. Suddenly the scale of everything in front of the little girl changed. The little stream now seemed like a mighty river and the model sloop a big, distant ship. And toward it, frightened, almost tumbling into the water, she reached out both arms and hastened along the

24

stream. "The captain got frightened," she thought to herself, hurrying after the toy which was floating away, in the hope that it would come to shore somewhere. Dragging the basket, which kept getting in the way, Asole exclaimed, "Oh, my heavens, what have I done!" And she kept trying not to lose sight of the lovely triangle of sail smoothly moving off into the distance. She stumbled, fell, got up, and ran on.

Asole had never been so deep into the forest. Absorbed in her eagerness to catch the toy, she had not looked about as she ran. There were many obstacles along the way: mossy trunks of fallen trees, holes, tall ferns, bushes such as sweetbrier and jasmine. These barred her way at every step. She gradually tired and stopped more and more often to catch her breath or to wipe sticky spider webs from her face. At times thickets of rushes and reeds completely hid the scarlet gleam of the sails, and Asole only caught sight of them again when she rounded a bend in the stream. Once she looked around and the face of the dense, many-colored forest, from the smoky pillars of light which penetrated the foliage to dark fissures of slumbering gloom, astonished the little girl. Awed for a moment, she quickly remembered the toy and ran on with all her strength.

An entire hour had passed in this seemingly futile, anxious pursuit when with surprise and relief Asole saw that the trees ahead were thinning out to reveal an expanse of the sea, white clouds, and a stretch of yellow sand onto which she ran, nearly stumbling with fatigue. Here was the mouth of the stream. Spreading out not very broadly and so shallow one could see through the streaming azure to the stones on its bed, it melted into the oncoming ocean waves. From the low bluff, pockmarked with roots, Asole saw that at the stream's edge, on a big flat stone, with his back to her, there sat a man holding the toy sloop in his hands. He was looking it over carefully from all sides with the same curiosity that an elephant might show toward a butterfly. Partially reassured by the fact that the toy was still in one piece, Asole clambered down the bluff. Coming up close behind the stranger, she studied him carefully, waiting for him to look up. But the stranger was so absorbed in contemplation of the surprise that had come from out of nowhere that the little girl had time to inspect him carefully and to decide that he was unlike anyone she had ever seen.

Before her was none other than Egl, the famous wandering collector of songs, legends, traditions, and folk stories. Gray curls dangled from under his straw hat. A gray blouse, tucked into dark blue trousers, and high boots gave him the look of a hunter. A white collar, a necktie, a buckle studded with silver, a cane, and a pouch with a new nickel lock, all these indicated a city dweller. A nose, lips, and eyes peered from a luxuriant growth of beard and a handlebar mustache. A kind of faded pallor would have dominated his features had it not been for eyes as gray as sand and as bright as shining steel which looked out at one with a bold, firm gaze.

"All right, now you can give it back to me," exclaimed the little girl bravely. "You've played with it enough. How did you manage to catch it?"

Egl raised his head and at once dropped the little boat, so surprised was he by the unexpected voice. The old chap studied her for a minute, smiled, and slowly ran his large hand, marked by heavy veins, through his beard. The calico dress she wore was faded from many washings, and it didn't even reach the knees of her thin, sunburned legs.

Her thick dark locks, which had been tied up in a lace kerchief, had tumbled down over her shoulders. The expression of her face was as airy and clean-cut as the flight of a swallow. The touch of sad questioning in her dark eyes made them somewhat older than the rest of her face. Its slightly asymmetrical oval had the kind of lovely sun-flush that comes only to a healthy, fair skin. Her tiny, half-open mouth shone with a gentle smile.

"I swear by the Brothers Grimm, Aesop, and Hans Christian Andersen," proclaimed Egl, with his eyes darting back and forth from the little girl to the toy sloop, "this is something special! Listen here, you little weed! Is this yours?"

"I ran after it all the way down the stream, till I thought I would die. It was right here?"

"At my very feet. A shipwreck which gives me, as beach pirate, the chance to offer you my booty. This sloop, abandoned by its crew, was cast up on the sand by a five-inch wave between my left heel and the tip of my walking stick." He thumped the ground with his cane. "And what's your name, little one?"

"Asole," she said, placing the toy Egl handed her back into her basket.

"Very good," continued the old man in his strange manner, without taking his eyes from her. In their depths gleamed a smile of friendliness. "There was no real reason to ask your name. I like it because it is so unusual, so musical, and also all in one tone like the whistle of an arrow, or the roar of a sea shell. Wouldn't it have been awful if you had told me you had one of those fine-sounding but intolerably ordinary names so out-of-tune with the Beautiful Unknown? I have no wish to know who you are, who your parents are, or where you live. Why disturb enchantment? Here I was sitting on this rock comparing Finnish and Japanese folk themes. And out of nowhere the stream cast up this toy sloop, and right after it you appeared. Just as you are. And I, my dear, am a poet at heart, even if I have never written any poetry of my own. What do you have there in your basket?"

"Toy boats," said Asole, shaking her basket. "There is also a steamer and three little houses with flags, where soldiers live."

"Very good. You were sent to sell them. On the way you began to play. You put the sloop into the water to sail a bit and it sailed away. Is that right?"

"How could you have seen?" Asole asked doubtingly, trying to remember whether she hadn't told him herself, "Did someone tell you? Or did you guess?"

"I knew."

"How?"

"Because I am—the chief of all the sorcerers."

Asole started. Her uneasiness, when she heard

Egl's words, bordered on fright. The deserted seashore, the absolute quiet, the exhausting chase for the sailboat, the strange words of the old man with sparkling eyes, his majestic beard and hair were beginning to create a confusion between reality and the supernatural in the mind of the small girl. If even for one second Egl had made a face or raised his voice, she would have fled in tears and panic. But Egl had already noticed how wide her eyes were.

"Don't be afraid of me," he said seriously. "In fact I want to speak to you frankly."

He had just defined to his own satisfaction exactly what there was in the girl's face that had so insistently etched itself on his mind. It was the unconscious expectation of a beautiful, a blessed destiny, he had decided. Oh why had he not been born a writer? What a glorious theme!

In Egl the instinct for the creation of legends, a result of his profession, was stronger than the need for caution in casting onto unknown soil the seeds of a great day-dream. Having begun, he had to continue:

"Come here, Asole, and listen to me with care. I have just come from that village in which you no doubt live, Caperna. I love folk tales and songs and I sat there a whole day in that village waiting to hear something new, a story I had not heard before. But there in your village they tell no legends, and they sing no songs. And if they do relate anything at all, it's, as one might expect, one of those familiar anecdotes about shrewd peasants and soldiers, glorifying cheating and thievery. If they sing anything at all, they chant silly ditties as dirty as unwashed feet and as crude as stomach rumblings, with awful tunes. But I've gone off the track. I'll have to begin again."

Pausing a moment, he continued:

"I really don't know how many years will go by, but in Caperna a legend will come to flower that will be remembered a long time. You will be grown, Asole. And one day, far out to sea, the sun will shine upon a white ship with scarlet sails. The white ship will slice through the waves and move right toward you. The miracle ship will sail silently forward without shouts or shots.

On the shore many people will be gathered, exclaiming in astonishment. You will be there too. The ship will approach majestically amidst the sounds of beautiful music. A fast skiff, gilded and decorated as for a holiday, with oriental rugs and flowers will be lowered from it. 'Why have you come? Whom do you want?' the people on the shore will ask. Just then you will see a bold and handsome prince. He will reach out his arms to you. 'Hello, Asole!' he will say. 'In a faraway land I saw you in my dreams and I have come to take you away with me forever to my kingdom. You will live there with me in a deep valley of roses. You will have everything you wish for. We will live together, you and I, in such friendship and joy that you will never know tears or sadness.' Then he will help you into the skiff, take you to his ship, and you will leave forever for a splendid country where the sun will rise and the stars will descend from the heavens to greet you when you come."

"All this will happen to me?" the little girl asked quietly.

Her serious eyes grew gay and shone with

faith. If the sorcerer were dangerous he wouldn't talk like that. This was clear. She drew closer to him.

"Perhaps it's already here—that ship?"

"Oh no, not yet," Egl said. "First, as I told you, you must grow up. And only then . . . How shall I say it? *It will happen.* That's all there is to it. And what will you do then?"

"I?" and she looked down into her basket but evidently she found nothing there which she considered a good enough gift for Egl. "I would love him," she declared quickly and added hesitating slightly, "that is, if he doesn't fight."

"No, he won't fight," declared the sorcerer, winking in a knowing way. "That he won't do— that I'll guarantee. Run along, little girl, and don't you forget what I've told you. Run along and peace be on your tender head!"

Longren was working in his vegetable patch, digging trenches for his potato plants. Lifting his head, he saw Asole running toward him with a glad and eager face.

"Oh, please," she panted, and took hold of

her father's work apron with both hands. "Listen to what happened. Over there on the seashore there's a sorcerer."

The rush of thoughts made it difficult for her to tell her story from the beginning. She began with the sorcerer and his wonderful prophecy. Then she described his appearance, and having reversed the whole order of things, finally got to the toy sloop which had sailed away from her.

Longren listened to the little girl without interrupting her and without smiling. By the time she had finished, his imagination had swiftly drawn for him a picture of an unknown old man with a bottle in one hand and the toy sloop in the other. He was about to turn away but remembered in time that events as important as this in the life of a child must be treated seriously. He nodded his head solemnly and declared: "Well, well! It would certainly seem that this man could only have been a sorcerer. I wish I could have had a look at him myself. But when you go to town again, don't stray from the road. You might get lost in the forest."

Throwing aside his spade, he seated himself on a low wooden fence and put the girl on his lap. Despite her tiredness, she tried to round out the details of her story, but the heat, excitement, and fatigue had made her sleepy. Her eyelids drooped. Her head slipped down on her father's strong shoulder. One second more and she would have been carried off into the Land of Nod, when suddenly, alarmed by a sudden doubt, Asole sat bolt upright, eyes closed, her small hands tightly gripping Longren's waistcoat. She exclaimed, "Will the sorcerer's ship really come for me?"

"It will come," the sailor answered quietly. "Since it's been promised you, it will come."

"She'll grow up and forget all about it," he thought to himself. "And for now she shouldn't have such a toy taken away from her. After all, little girl, the future will show you many a sail, not scarlet, but dirty and evil. From a distance they'll look grand and white but close by they will be torn and coarse. A passerby had his joke with my little daughter. Oh, well! A fine joke! Quite a joke! See how exhausted you are, half a day in the woods, in the heart of the forest. You'll have your scarlet sails."

Asole slept. Longren, pulling out his pipe with his free hand, lit up, and the breeze carried the smoke through the wattle fence at the end of the garden into a bush on the other side of it. Beside the bush with his back to the fence sat a young beggar chewing on a roll. He was in a jolly mood, having been amused by the conversation between father and daughter, and the tobacco smell aroused his greed.

"Give a poor man something to smoke," he said through the fence. "My tobacco compared to yours is simply poison."

"I'd be glad to," Longren answered in a half-whisper, "but my tobacco is in my pocket and I don't want to wake up my daughter to get it."

"Big to-do! So she'll wake up and go back to sleep again and a passerby will have a smoke."

"No," said Longren. "It isn't as if you have no tobacco at all. The child is tired out. Come back, if you like, later on."

The beggar spat contemptuously. He took up his bag and hung it on his stick:

"Some princess she is! You've sure got those foreign ships stuck in her head! Cranky crank and big boss too!"

"Listen, you!" whispered Longren. "I will wake her up, and just in order to break your big neck. Get out!"

Half an hour later the beggar sat in the local tavern at a table with a dozen fishermen. Behind them, pulling at their husbands' drinking arms and sometimes even grabbing the mugs for a drink themselves, sat great, buxom women, as rounded as cobblestones, with bushy brows and arms thick as logs. The beggar was boiling with outrage as he spoke.

"So he refused me tobacco. 'When you come of age,' he tells her, 'then there'll come a special red ship. For you. It's your lot to marry a prince. So just believe in that sorcerer.' And I say: 'Wake her up, wake her up, and get me some tobacco.' And then he chased me half the way here."

"Who? What? What's he talking about?" questioned the curious women.

The fishermen, hardly turning their heads,

gabbled, half laughing, "Longren and his daughter have really gone wild. Maybe they're soft in the head. The man says that apparently some magician was at their place. They're waiting—listen, you old girls, here's one for you—for a foreign prince and a ship with red sails."

Three days later on the way back from the shop in Lisse, Asole heard for the first time: "Hey you, you witch! Asole! Look over there! See the red sails!"

The trembling little girl involuntarily shaded her eyes with her palm and peered out at the ocean. Then she turned in the direction of the taunts. Twenty steps away from her stood a pack of urchins. They made faces and stuck out their tongues at her. Sobbing, she ran home.

GREY

Julius Caesar believed it was better to be first in a small Iberian village than second in Rome. And Arthur Grey took Caesar at his word. He wanted to be a sea captain, and became a sea captain.

The enormous house in which Arthur was born was gloomy indoors and majestic outside. It was surrounded by a flower garden and a private park. In whimsical strings, tulips of the rarest shades, silver blue, violet, and touched with rose, wound through the well-kept lawn. Ancient trees slumbered in diffused half-light above the rushes of a winding stream. The castle fence—for this was a real castle—consisted of twisting cast-iron pillars joined together by iron grillwork. Each pillar was topped by a luxuriant cast-iron lily, and on holidays the lily cups were filled with oil and served as lamps which blazed out into the darkness in a long and fiery array.

Grey's father and mother were the haughty prisoners of their position, wealth, and the laws of the society to which they belonged. One part of their beings was occupied by a gallery of ancestors, little worthy of having had their portraits painted, and the other was filled with the hoped-for continuation of the gallery beginning with little Arthur. He was thus predestined to live out his life according to a fixed plan and to die in such a way that his portrait could hang on the wall without offense to family honor. There was one small hitch to this plan. Arthur Grey was born with a lively mind of his own and was not in the least inclined to continue along the lines of family precedent.

This vitality and the contrariness of the boy began to be apparent when he was eight. The knight-errant of whimsy, the explorer and the miracle-worker, in other words that person who chooses from among the infinite variety of roles in life, the most dangerous—that of the hero— came to the fore in Grey on the day he pushed a chair up against a wall so as to be able to reach up to a painting showing the crucifixion.

He removed the nails driven through Christ's bleeding hands by covering them over with blue paint pilfered from a house painter. He found the painting more bearable in this condition. He was about to paint over the nails in the feet when his father took him by surprise. The old man helped him off the chair by the ear and asked, "Why did you spoil the painting?"

"I didn't spoil it."

"It's the work of a famous artist."

"I don't care," said young Grey. "I won't have nails sticking out of hands and blood running. I don't want it."

In his son's reply Lionel Grey recognized himself. He hid his smile behind his mustache and did not punish him.

Young Grey searched the castle incessantly and made astonishing discoveries. In the garret he found discarded knights' armor, books bound in iron and leather, rotted clothing, and a big flock of doves. In the cellar he acquired an interesting knowledge of Madeira, sherry, and other wines. Here in the dim light of sharp-pointed windows, resting beneath the weight of the slanting triangles of stone archways, stood large and small barrels. The largest, with its flat end against the back of the cellar, took up the entire wall. The century-old dark oak of the barrel shone as if polished. Among the smaller casks stood fat-bellied bottles of green or dark blue glass in woven covers. On the earthen floor between the stones grew gray mushrooms on thin stalks. Everywhere there was mold, moss, dampness, and a sour, stifling odor. An enormous spider web glistened gold in the far corner when, just before twilight, the sun brightened it with a last ray. There was also the spot where two casks of the finest Alicante of the times of Cromwell were buried. The wine keeper, Poldychoke, as he pointed out the corner to Grey, took the opportunity of repeating the story of this famous wine. Before beginning his account, Poldychoke did not fail to make sure that the spigot of the big barrel was functioning properly. And, indeed, as he continued his story, he went back to check again and again. One could see when he returned, from the involun-

44

tary tears of satisfaction that moistened his merry eyes, that his heart was obviously lighter.

"Well, here's the way it is," Poldychoke said to Grey, as he seated himself on an empty box and shoved snuff up his sharp nose. "Look over there. Just for one little glass of the wine buried there, many a drinker would let his tongue be cut out. Each of the barrels contains one hundred quarts of a substance that can make the soul explode and turn the body into stiff dough. Its color is darker than cherry. It is as thick as the thickest cream, so thick it will not pour from a bottle. It is encased in casks of ebony that are as strong as iron, and they are banded by double hoops of red copper. Engraved on the hoops in Latin are the words, 'Grey will drink me down when he is in paradise.' This legend has been interpreted in many ways. Your great-grandfather, Simeon Grey, tried to trick fate by building himself a country residence and calling it Paradise. But guess what happened? The old gourmet got so excited he died of a heart attack just as they started to remove the hoops. Since then no one has touched the casks, and it is believed that to drink the precious wine will bring unhappiness.

"These casks were brought here by your ancestor, John Grey of Lisbon, on the good ship *Beagle* in 1793. Two thousand gold piasters were paid for them. The legend on the casks was inscribed by the master armorer, Benjamin Elyan, of Pondicherry. The casks are buried in the earth to a depth of six feet and covered over with the ashes of grape vines. This wine has never been drunk, and never will be drunk.

"I will drink it," said Grey, stamping his foot.

"That's a bold chap!" exclaimed Poldychoke. "Are you going to drink it in paradise?"

"Of course. This is paradise! I have it right here, see?" And Grey laughed quietly, opening his palm. The tender yet firm lines were lit up by the sun, and the small boy closed his fingers into a fist. "Here it is right in here! Now it's here and now it's gone."

As he spoke, he opened and closed his hand, and finally, pleased with his joke, ran out ahead of Poldychoke and up the dark stairway into the corridor of the ground floor.

The kitchen was strictly forbidden territory to Grey. But once he had discovered its world of blazing hearth, fires, of steam, soot, and sizzle, of bubbling and boiling liquids, of clattering knives, of delicious smells, the boy went often to the enormous room. The cooks moved about in silence like oracles. Their white kitchen bonnets outlined against the background of blackened walls endowed their work with the solemnity of a religious service. The merry fat dishwashers at the water barrels rinsed the dishes to the ringing of china and silver. Small boys, bending beneath their heavy loads, carried in full baskets of fish, oysters, crabs, and fruits. On the long table lay rainbow-colored pheasants, gray ducks, colorful chickens, and a pig's carcass with a short little tail and eyes shut like those of an infant. There were also turnips, cabbages, walnuts, black raisins, and suntanned peaches.

In the kitchen young Grey was a bit shy. It seemed to him as if here everything were ruled by dark, powerful forces, the mainspring of the life of the castle. Shouts sounded like commands and invocations. The movements of those working, thanks to long habit, had acquired a precision that seemed inspired. Grey was not yet tall enough to peer into the biggest pot of all, which seethed like Vesuvius, but he felt a special respect for it. With trepidation he watched it being stirred by two servants. Smoky foam splashed out on the hot stove, and steam, rising from it in waves, filled the kitchen. One time so much liquid splashed out that one of the kitchen maids scalded her arm. Her skin grew bright red immediately. Even her fingernails became crimson with the accumulation of blood, and Betsy, as she was called, wept and rubbed the burn with oil at the same time. The tears poured relentlessly down her round and frightened face.

Grey froze. While the women were bustling around Betsy, he felt for her suffering and wanted to understand her pain.

"Does it hurt a lot?" he asked.

"You just try it and you'll see," Betsy had replied, covering her arm with her apron.

The boy, frowning, climbed up on a stool, reached into the pot with a long spoon for some of the hot liquid—it was mutton soup—and dripped it on his hand. The sharp pain made him reel. White as flour, Grey went up to Betsy, sticking his stinging hand into his trouser pocket.

"I'm sure it hurts a lot," he said, saying nothing of his own experiment. "Let's go to the doctor, Betsy. Let's go!"

He pulled her energetically by the skirt, at the same time as the proponents of home remedies vied with each other in preparing recipes for her salvation. But the girl, in great torment, went along with Grey. The physician did ease the pain and dress the burn. Only after Betsy had left did Grey show his own hand.

This minor episode made twenty-year-old Betsy and ten-year-old Grey the best of friends. She kept stuffing his pockets with dumplings and apples. And he repeated to her fairy tales and other stories that he read in his books.

When he discovered that Betsy could not marry the stableboy, Jim, because they had no money to set up housekeeping, Grey broke open his porcelain piggy bank with the fireplace tongs and took out his savings amounting to about one hundred pounds. Rising early and waiting till dowryless Betsy had gone to work in the kitchen, he crept into her room and hid his gift in the girl's trunk. With it he left a note which said: "Betsy, this is for you. From the Chief of the Brigands, Robin Hood." There was a big fuss in the kitchen over the incident. Finally Grey had to come forward and confess. But he refused either to take the money back or to say anything more about it.

His mother was one of those persons whom life casts in a ready-made mold. She lived in a semi-slumber, lulled by a security that provided for every wish of her rather mediocre person. She had nothing to do at all, except consult her seamstress, her doctor, and her butler. But her passionate, almost religious, attachment to her strange child was, it would seem, the one outlet for good instincts otherwise so anaesthetized by her upbringing and fate that they were no longer really active, leaving her without any real will of her own. She resembled a hen who had hatched a swan's egg. She was pained by the beautiful strangeness of her son. Sadness, love, and constraint welled up in her when she pressed the boy to her breast. Her heart did not speak the same language as her conventional tongue.

This lady of high society, who could respond only with icy silence to the fiery appeals of life, whose delicate beauty repelled rather than attracted because it reflected a haughty constraint which was totally lacking in femininity, when left alone with her son became an ordinary mama who spoke in loving, gentle tones those heartfelt trivialities which cannot be put down on paper. She could not say No to her son at all. She forgave him everything: his visits to the kitchen, his dislike for his lessons, his disobedience, and his innumerable whims.

If he didn't want the trees pruned, they remained unpruned. If he asked that someone be forgiven or rewarded, it was done. He could ride any horse he wanted to, bring into the castle any stray dog, rummage about in the library, run barefoot, and eat whatever he felt like eating.

For a time his father fought against this, but in the end he gave in to his wife's wishes. He did, however, take one precautionary measure. The servants' children were removed from the castle because he feared that association with them might change what were a boy's caprices into permanent tastes that would be hard to up-root. He was, in general, occupied to the exclusion of everything else with innumerable family lawsuits whose origin dated back to the discovery of paper, and which would probably continue until the death of all pettifoggers and intriguers. In addition, affairs of state, business dealings in connection with his inheritance, the dictation of his memoirs, formal hunts, the reading of newspapers, and complex correspondence kept him away from his family. He saw his son so rarely that he sometimes forgot how old he was.

Thus young Arthur Grey lived in his own

world. He played alone, usually in the rear courtyards of the castle which in olden times had been used for military purposes. These broad vacant lots, with remnants of deep moats and stone powder magazines overgrown with moss, were now fields of tall weeds, nettles, burdock, thorn bushes, and modest, varicolored flowers. Grey spent hours investigating mole holes, fighting the tall weeds, catching butterflies, and building fortresses out of broken brick, which he then bombarded with sticks and cobblestones.

He was twelve when in one supreme moment all the inner urgings of his spirit, all the undirected traits of his character, his secret aspirations, became fused into one unconquerable desire.

It happened in the library. Its high door, the upper part of which was made of translucent glass, was usually kept locked. But the bolt was loose, and if one pressed hard enough, it would shift a bit and could, with an effort, be forced open. When the spirit of adventure pushed Arthur Grey into invading the library, he was astonished by the dusty light which reflected the glowing pattern of the stained glass that adorned the upper part of the windows. The silence of solitude lay here. Some of the dark rows of bookcases were joined onto the windows, half cutting off their light. In the aisles between the bookcases were piles of books: an open album, with loose pages scattered about; scrolls tied with gold cord; stacks of gloomy-looking volumes; thick layers of manuscripts; an embankment of miniature books that crackled crisply when opened. There were drawings on tables, rows of new editions, maps; a variety of bindings, crude, soft, black, many-hued, dark blue, gray, thick, thin, rough, and smooth. The shelves were tightly packed with books. They seemed like walls enclosing life itself in their thickness. In the reflection of the glass-enclosed bookcases, one saw other shelves which seemed to be splattered with colorless, shining spots. An enormous globe encircled in a spherical brass cross of the equator and meridian stood on a round table.

When he turned to leave, Grey saw hanging

over the door an enormous painting whose power immediately permeated the mustiness of the library. It showed a ship, streams of foam flowing along its sides. It was at the very peak of rise on the crest of a mighty wave and seemed to be coming straight at the onlooker. Its bowsprit, lifted high, hid the base of the mast. The crest of the wave, sliced by the keel, resembled the wings of a giant bird. Foam hung in the air. The sails, partly hidden behind the forecastle and bowsprit, were filled with the furious force of a storm. They lay backwards, in their full expanse, readying themselves to top the wave, straighten, and go forward, over the chasm ahead, driving the ship into new maelstroms. Tatters of clouds hovered over the ocean. The dim light of evening struggled hopelessly to stem the onrushing darkness of the night. But the most remarkable thing of all in this picture was the figure of a man standing on the forecastle, his back to the onlooker. In him was personified not only the entire situation, but the essence of that exact moment. Although in itself the man's pose—feet astride and arms waving—

did not explain what he was doing, it conveyed an intense concentration directed at something on the deck, invisible to the viewer. The turned-up flaps of his long kaftan shook in the wind. His white braid and a black sword were flung back into the air. The lavishness of his uniform indicated he was the captain, and the balancing stance of his body pointed up the force of the wave. He wore no cap, and evidently completely absorbed in the danger of the moment, he was shouting—but what? Had he seen someone go overboard and given the order to come about? Or was he calling to the boatswain and trying to outshout the wind? Not actual thoughts but echoes of thoughts invaded Grey's mind as he looked at the painting. Suddenly he felt as if someone unknown and invisible had come up to him on his left and was standing beside him. All he had to do was to turn his head and the sensation would disappear. Grey knew this, but instead of silencing his imagination he listened to it. A soundless voice shouted some phrases, incomprehensible, as if in Malayan. He heard the rolling roar of long, drawn-out avalanches. An echo and a dark wind filled the library. All of this young Grey heard within himself. He looked around. Instantly the quiet silenced the noisy maze of fantasy. Communication with the storm was lost.

Several times Grey came back to look at the painting. It became for him the key word in the dialogue between his dreams and life and helped him to understand himself. The broad sea became a part of the small boy. He rummaged in the library, searching for and reading greedily those books behind whose golden doors there stretched the blue sheen of the ocean. In this sea, foam running astern, ships sailed. Some of them lost their sails, their masts, and devoured by the waves, descended into the darkness of the deep amidst the twinkling phosphorescent eyes of fish. Others, in the grip of breakers, broke on reefs. The subsiding force of the waves dangerously tossed a wrecked hull back and forth. The abandoned ship, with torn and broken rigging, lived through a long agony until a new storm broke it into bits.

Others loaded successfully in one port and unloaded in another. The crew, at the tavern table, praised the life of the sea and gaily gulped down their drinks. There were pirate ships flying a Jolly Roger and with an awesome knife-bearing crew; ghost ships gleaming with deathly blue light; navy ships with soldiers, cannons, and music; ships of scientific expeditions looking for volcanoes, for marine plants and animals; ships with dark secrets and mutinies; ships of discovery and ships of adventure.

In this world of the sea, naturally the figure of the captain rose high above everyone else. He was the fate, the heart, the brain of his ship. He determined the crew's play and work. He picked the crew himself and he answered largely for its shortcomings. He knew the habits and family affairs of the ship's men. In the eyes of his subordinates he was the possessor of magic knowledge, thanks to which he could sail with assurance through boundless expanses from Lisbon to Shanghai. He coped with a storm by a complex system of countermeasures and quieted panic with his curt orders. He sailed and he stopped where he wished. He directed departures and loadings, repairs and rest time. His enormous and wisely applied power, employed as it was in work full of incessant movement, was hard to imagine. Such authority, self-contained and total, was equaled only by the power of a God.

Such was the mental picture of a captain, such the image of his position that took hold of Grey's consciousness, his spiritual life. There is no other profession that can so perfectly fuse into a whole all of the treasures of life and at the same time keep inviolate the highly delicate pattern of each separate joy. Danger, risk, the power of nature, the light of a far country, the wonderful unknown, love budding and flowering in meeting and parting, the fascination of encounters, persons, events, immeasurable variety, and rising on the horizon the Southern Cross, the Big Dipper, and all the continents —all these are within range of a captain's sharp eyes. And yet his cabin is full of the homeland which never leaves him, with its books, pictures, letters, and dried flowers tied with a silken curl and resting in a suede pouch on a firm chest.

In the fall of his fifteenth year, young Grey ran away to sea. The schooner *Anselm* sailed from the port of Dubelt for Marseille, carrying on board a ship's boy with small hands and the soft features of a girl. The ship's boy was Grey, who had come aboard wearing patent leather boots as thin as gloves, cambric linens embroidered with the sign of a crown, and a fine traveling bag.

During a year while the *Anselm* visited France, America, and Spain, young Grey squandered part of his assets on pastry, by this token paying tribute to the past. The remainder, in the name of the present and the future, he lost at cards. He wanted to be a real devil of a seafaring man. He drank down liquor, nearly choking. When he swam, he dove, head first, into the water, with a sinking heart, from a fifteen foot height. Little by little he lost everything he had brought with him—except his strange, soaring spirit. He lost his frailty and became broad of bone and strong of muscle. A dark tan replaced his pallor. The once refined carelessness of his movements took on the precision of the working hand. In his thoughtful eyes there appeared a gleam like that of a person staring into a fire. His manner of speaking, after it lost its uneven, haughty, shy fluidity, became curt and exact.

The captain of the *Anselm* was a good man but a strict sailor, who had taken the boy aboard out of caprice. He saw in young Grey's desperate desire to go to sea only an eccentric wish and gloated when he imagined how, in a month or so, the boy would say to him, without being able to look him in the eye: "Captain Hopp, I've scratched my elbows climbing about on the rigging. My side and my back ache. My fingers won't bend any longer. My head is splitting, and my legs are shaking. All of those wet ships' cables that weigh almost a hundred-weight suspended in one's hands, those jackstays, shrouds, windlasses, hawsers, topmasts, and crosstrees, the whole lot of them were created solely to torture my tender body. I want to go home to my mother."

Listening in his mind to this speech, Captain Hopp imagined how he would reply: "You just go wherever you please, my little chick. If your tender little wings have got a little tar on them, you can wash it off at home with Rosa-Mimosa Eau-de-Cologne."

The name for the eau-de-cologne, which Hopp had thought up himself, made him laugh in his thoughts louder than anything else, and when he had delivered his fare-thee-well, he would repeat out loud to himself: "Yes, yes, run along to your 'Rosa-Mimosa.'"

As time went on, this dialogue came to the mind of the captain less and less. Grey worked steadily toward his goal, with teeth gritted and face pale. He bore the nerve-wracking labor with a determined exertion of will, knowing that the more the severity of life on the ship penetrated his being, the easier things would become for him, and his awkwardness would be replaced by skill. It happened now and then that he was knocked down by a loop in the anchor chain and driven against the deck, that a ship's cable which slipped off the bollard tore out of his hands and burned the flesh from his palms, that he was hit in the face with a corner of a wet sail that had iron cables sewn into it. To sum it up, at first all the work was a trial and torture which demanded the sharpest of attention. But no matter how hard he breathed and how difficult it was to bend, a smile of contempt never left his lips. He bore in silence the laughter, mockery, and inevitable cursing until he became a "native" in this new orbit of life. And from then on he replied to each insult with a blow of the fist.

Once when Captain Hopp observed how skillfully Grey had tied a sail to the yardarm, he said to himself: "Well, you rogue, you've won." When Grey returned to the deck, Hopp called him into his cabin and, opening a well-worn book, said: "Listen carefully. Stop smoking! We're going to turn this puppy into a captain."

And he began to read, rather one should say shout, from the book the ancient terminology of the sea. This was Grey's first lesson. Over the period of a year he learned navigation, ship-building, admiralty law, how to read sailing directions, and bookkeeping. Captain Hopp shook his hand and addressed him as an equal.

In Vancouver, Grey found a letter waiting from his mother. It abounded in tears and worry. He replied: "I understand. But if you were only to look at things as I do! Try to see them with my eyes. If you could only hear things as I do! Take a sea shell and put it to your ear, for it holds the roar of an eternal wave. If only you could love a smile as I do—for there is everything in your letter except love and a human being."

He sailed with the *Anselm* until it arrived with a cargo at Dubelt. Taking advantage of the stop, the twenty-year-old Grey went ashore to visit the castle.

All was the same as it had been five years before. Only the foliage of the young elms had become more lush, and the pattern which their shadow cast on the facade of the castle had grown denser and broader.

The servants who ran out to meet him were happy but startled. They froze into the same attitude of respect with which what seemed no longer ago than yesterday they had greeted the other Grey, his father.

They told him where to find his mother. He entered her high-ceilinged room and closed the door quietly behind him. He stopped motionless, looking at the woman in a black dress whose hair had turned gray. She stood before a crucifix. Her passionate whisper resounded like a heartbeat. "Oh, for those at sea, for travelers, for those ill, and for those suffering and for those in prison," Grey heard, holding his breath. "And for my son . . ."

"I am here," and he could say nothing more. His mother turned. She had become thin. The haughtiness of her narrow face gave way to a new expression which seemed to bring back her youth. She walked swiftly to her son. A short laugh came from deep within her. There was a restrained exclamation, and the tears welled in her eyes. That was all. But in that moment she lived more intensely, more deeply, than at any time in her entire life. "I recognized you at once! Oh my darling, my little one!" And Grey ceased to be an adult.

She told him about his father's death, and then he told her about himself. She listened without reproach. But in what he had found to be the meaning of his life, the truth of his being, she saw only toys with which her little boy was amusing himself. Such toys as continents, oceans, ships.

Grey spent seven days at the castle. On the eighth he took a large sum of money and returned to Dubelt, where he met Captain Hopp. "Thank you," he said to the captain. "You have been a real friend. Farewell, my elder comrade." And he underscored the meaning of the word with a handshake as tight as a vise. "From now on I must sail on my own, on my own ship."

Hopp spat in a temper, pulled his hand free, and went off. But Grey caught up with him and embraced him. Then they went together to a tavern where they were joined by the

entire twenty-four-man crew of the *Anselm*.
They drank and ate everything on the buffet
and in the kitchen as well.

In a short time the evening star shone down
on a dream fulfilled in the port of Dubelt—*The
Secret,* a three-masted galiot of 260 tons, which
had been purchased by Grey. And so, captain
of his own ship, Arthur Grey sailed the seas for
four years more before fate took him to the port
of Lisse. But he never forgot how his mother
had greeted him, and twice each year he visited
the castle.

DAWN

Foam steaming astern, *The Secret* crossed the ocean, leaving a white wake behind it, and came to rest in the glow of the evening lights of Lisse. The ship was anchored in the harbor not far from the lighthouse. Ten days were spent unloading silk, coffee, and tea, and on the eleventh the crew went to relax at the tavern. On the twelfth day, for no reason at all, Grey fell into a deep melancholy.

In the morning, hardly awake, he already felt that the day had begun badly. He dressed gloomily, breakfasted without appetite, even forgot to read his newspaper, and sat smoking for a long time. His vague thoughts, nebulous desires, led nowhere. Finally he got down to business.

With the boatswain, Grey inspected the ship, ordered the shrouds tightened, the steering chain loosened a bit, the hawser-holes cleaned, the jib changed, the deck tarred, the compass polished, and the cabins opened, aired, and swept out. But his work failed to distract him. He could not rid himself of his uneasy gloom and went through the day glumly and irritably. It seemed as if someone had invited him out somewhere, but he had forgotten who had asked him and where he was to go.

In the evening he seated himself in his cabin, picked up a book, and spent a long time contradicting the writer and making paradoxical notes in the margins. This game, this argument with a dead author, amused him for a time. Then he picked up his pipe, and submerging himself in purple smoke, wandered among the ghostly images of his fancy.

Tobacco is a powerful thing. It can be like oil which is poured on troubled waters to pacify their fury. It mellows irritation. Under its influence disturbed feelings regain their harmony. After three pipefuls, Grey's melancholy finally lost its edge and was transformed into a meditative absorption. He remained in this state for about an hour more. When the fog of his mood had lifted and Grey returned to full consciousness, he felt like moving about a bit and went up on deck. It was the middle of the night. Over the side, the slumbering black water reflected the stars and the lights of the mast lanterns. The air, warm as a cheek, smelled of the sea. Grey, looking upward, squinted at the golden point of a star. Momentarily, from an infinity of distance, the fiery needle of a planet pierced his pupils. He listened to the subdued roar of the nighttime city located at the head of the gulf. Once in a while, from the shore, the wind and the sensitive water carried a phrase that sounded as if it had been spoken on deck. Resounding clearly, it was finally lost in the creaking of the rigging. On the forecastle a match flamed up, illuminating someone's fingers, round eyes, and a mustache. Grey whistled. The glowing embers of a pipe floated toward him. In the dark the captain made out the hands and face of the officer of the watch.

"Tell Letika," Grey said, "that he is to come with me. Tell him to bring the fishing tackle."

He descended into the ship's skiff where he waited ten minutes for Letika. This nimble sailor, after banging the oars against the side, handed them to Grey. He got into the boat, set the oars into their locks, and pushed a bag of provisions into the skiff's stern. Grey sat at the rudder.

"Where to, Captain?" asked Letika, turning the boat about with his right oar.

The captain remained silent. The sailor knew that when the captain wished to be silent no one else was to speak, and he rowed swiftly on.

Grey headed out to the open sea and then turned in along the left coast. It was all the same to him where he rowed. The rudder murmured softly. The oars tinkled and splashed. All the rest was sea and silence.

In the course of a day a person listens to such a multitude of thoughts, impressions, talk, and words, that put together it would constitute more than one fat book. The face of each day has its own particular expression, but Grey stared into the face of this day without recognizing it. Its troubled features revealed one of those moods that is the reflection of many, and cannot be pinned down. No matter how hard one tries to describe it, it remains beyond the realm of words and even of concepts, like the hint of a fragrance. Grey was in the power of just such an indefinable feeling. It's true he could have said to himself: "I'm expecting something to happen. I'll wait and see. I'll soon know. . . ." But that would have been as inadequate an expression of his feelings as are the sketches of mere sections of an architectural concept. Yet in all these hidden murmurings there was the promise of some bright excitement.

On the left, in the direction they were rowing, the shoreline loomed up as a wavy thickening of the darkness. Above bright windows floated sparks from chimneys. This was Caperna. Grey heard squabbling and barking. The lights of the village were like the burning holes in a stove door through which the flaming coal can be seen. On the right lay the ocean, as clear, as distinct, as the presence of a sleeping man. After passing Caperna, Grey headed for the shore. They landed quietly. Lighting his lantern, Grey carefully examined the pools at the foot of a cliff and its highest projection above. The place attracted him.

"Here we will fish," he said, clapping the oarsman on the shoulder.

"This is the first time I've ever sailed with a captain like this one," the sailor muttered to himself. "This captain is businesslike, yet not like the rest. He's a tough captain. Anyway I like him."

Pushing the oar down into the silt, he tied the boat to it. They both climbed up the cliff, clambering over stones which slipped from under their hands and feet. At the top they found a thicket. Soon the sound of chopping rose—an axe cutting through a dry tree trunk. After he had felled the tree, Letika started a bonfire on the cliff. Shadows darted and the reflection of the flame danced in the water. In the retreating darkness grass and branches glistened. Above the bonfire the intermingling air and smoke sparkled and quivered.

Grey seated himself at the fire.

"Here you are," he said, handing over the bottle. "Drink, my friend, Letika, to the health of all teetotalers. By the way, you've brought ginger wine instead of tonic."

"Excuse me, Captain," replied the sailor, taking a breath. "Do you mind if I have a bit to eat with my drink?" And he bit off part of a chicken. Then, taking the wingbone out of his mouth, he continued: "I know you prefer tonic. But it was dark and I was in a hurry. Ginger, you see, makes a man stronger. Whenever I'm likely to get into a fight, I take ginger."

While the captain was eating and drinking, the sailor watched him out of the corner of his eye. Then, unable to contain himself, he said, "Is it true what they say, Captain, that you are high born?"

"That's not an interesting subject, Letika. Take the fishing rod and fish if you want to."

"What about you?"

"Me? I'm not sure. Maybe. After a while . . ."

Letika unwound the string from the rod, all the while chanting in rhyme. He was a master

at this and the crew got enormous satisfaction
out of this trick of his.

"With a piece of string and pole of wood I've made
  myself a whip.
And now I tie a hook on it and, whistling, make it flip."

He poked about in the worm can with his
finger.

"This small worm, dug in the earth,
  he was alive and glad.
And now he's squirming on my hook,
  and by a fish will soon be had."

Finally he left, singing:

"Quiet the night,
The vodka is right.
Fear and tremble, little fish.
Letika wants you, in his dish."

Grey lay down near the fire, watching its reflection in the water. He was daydreaming,
without making any effort to direct his imagin-
ings. In such a state, though absent-mindedly
aware of his surroundings, a person sees them
only vaguely. His thoughts rush like a horse into
a closely packed crowd, first pressing, pushing
asunder, and then stopping. Emptiness, dismay,

and restraint by turn accompany them. They roam about in the heart of things, hastening from exhilaration to clandestine urgings. They circle through the earth and the heavens, speak volubly with imagined persons, deaden or exaggerate recollections. In this cloudlike movement everything is lively and puffed up and not connected, as in a delirium. And often the relaxed consciousness smiles at seeing how suddenly, like a guest, a completely irrelevant image appears. This was Grey's state of mind as he watched the fire; he was "somewhere else," not there.

The elbow on which he leaned, supporting his head with his hand, became damp and went to sleep. The stars shone faintly. The darkness became denser with the tension preceding sunrise. The captain was getting sleepy. He wanted to take a drink and reached for the water pouch, but was already dreaming before he could untie it. Then he stopped dreaming. When he awoke after two hours, it seemed to Grey only seconds since he had placed his head down upon his arms. Letika had come twice to the fire, had smoked and looked with curiosity into the mouths of the fish he had caught. But he had found nothing there.

For a moment Grey forgot how he had come to this place. With astonishment he saw the glow of the morning, the cliff on the coast among bright branches, and the dark blue distance. Above the horizon and at the same time close to his feet, hung the leaves of a hazelnut tree. Below the cliff the surf hissed—as if it were right at Grey's back. From the glistening leaves, drops of dew fell with a cold plop on his sleepy face. He got up. Light was triumphing over darkness everywhere. The dying embers of the fire clung to life with a thin wisp of smoke. Grey savored the smell of the fire mingling with the breath of forest greenery.

Letika wasn't there. He had gotten carried away by his fishing. Perspiring, he was angling with the concentration of a gambler. Grey emerged from the thicket behind the cliff into bushes scattered along the incline of a hill. The grass smoked and burned in the dawn light. The wet flowers looked like children forcibly washed with cold water. It was difficult for Grey to push through the dense green world, breathing with its infinite number of tiny mouths. The captain forced his way to an open spot overgrown with variegated grass. There he saw a sleeping girl.

He quietly pushed back a branch with his hand and stood still with a feeling of dangerous discovery. No more than five steps away from him, curled up, with one leg bent and the other stretched out, her head on her cosily upturned hands, lay Asole. Her hair was pushed back in disarray. The button at her neck was undone, disclosing a white hollow. Her skirt was crumpled up, showing her knees. Her eyelashes slept on her cheeks in the shadow of a gently rounded temple half-covered by a dark lock of hair. The little finger of her right hand bent beneath the back of her head. Grey squatted down and stared at the girl's face.

Perhaps in other circumstances this girl would have been noticed by him only because of her eyes. But here he saw her from a different point of view. Everything in him smiled, everything was moved. Of course, he didn't know her and he didn't know her name. Nor could he know why she had fallen asleep here in the meadow. But he was satisfied with things as they were. He loved pictures without legends and signatures. The impression was incomparably stronger. Content, unfettered by words, becomes limitless, confirming all guesses, all dreams.

The shade of the foliage inched closer to the tree trunks, but Grey remained sitting in his uncomfortable position. Everything about the girl was asleep. Her dark hair slept. Her dress and its pleats slept. Even the grass near her body was slumbering out of sympathy, or so it seemed.

Letika had long since called out, "Captain, where are you?" But the captain had not heard him.

When at last Grey stood up, his bent for the unusual inspiring him to an impulse, he removed from his finger an ancient and precious ring and carefully placed it on the little finger which gleamed white from beneath the back of the girl's head. The finger moved impatiently and drooped. After looking once again at the girl's sleeping face, Grey turned and in the bushes behind him saw Letika, his eyebrows raised high. The sailor, with mouth open, stared at Grey with perhaps the same look of astonishment that had been Jonah's when he had gazed into the yawning jaws of his completely furnished whale.

"Ah, it's you, Letika!" said Grey. "Look at her. Lovely, isn't she?"

"A divine painting," exclaimed the sailor in a stage whisper. He loved to repeat bookish phrases. "In consideration of the circumstances there is a certain something that disposes one favorably. I caught four small fish—and something else thick as a bladder."

"Quiet, Letika. Let's get away from here."

They went off into the bushes. They reached the turn which would take them down to the boat, but Grey stopped to study the low shoreline in the distance where, above the greenery and the sand, the morning smoke poured from the chimneys of Caperna. In the smoke he saw the image of the girl.

Then, with determination, he turned away from the direction of the boat and descended the slope toward the village. The sailor followed without questioning him. He knew, as always, that the time had come for obligatory silence. When they came close to the first buildings, Grey suddenly asked, "Can you tell, Letika, with your experienced eye, where the local tavern is?"

"It ought to be that black rooftop over there," Letika said. "But then again, maybe it isn't."

"What's so special about that roof?"

"I wouldn't be able to say, Captain. It's nothing more than the voice of my heart."

They went up to the house, which was in fact Manners' inn. Through the open window a bottle could be seen on the table. Next to it someone's dirty hand was pulling on his half-gray mustache.

Even though it was still early, there were already three people in the main taproom of the inn. At the window sat a coalman, owner of the already noted mustache. Between the buffet and the inner door of the taproom, eating scrambled eggs and beer, sat two fishermen. Hin Manners, a tall young fellow, with a dull freckled face and that special expression of sly impertinence in his near-sighted eyes that is characteristic of hucksters and hawkers in general, was wiping glasses and dishes behind the bar. The sun had cast the shadow of the window frames on the dirty floor.

No sooner had Grey stepped into the area of smoky light than Manners, bowing respectfully, had come forward. He had immediately sensed that Grey was a real captain, a rank rarely seen in this village. Grey ordered some rum. Covering the table with a tablecloth yellow from long use, Manners brought out a bottle, but only after licking and sticking back the edge of the label which had started to peel off. He returned behind the bar, attentively watching, in turn, Grey and the plate he himself was scraping.

As Letika, his glass held in both hands, was quietly whispering to Grey and at the same time looking out of the window, the captain motioned Manners to come over. Hin, with a self-satisfied expression, seated himself on the edge of a chair, flattered that he was being addressed, and especially because he had been summoned by the conspiratorial crook of a finger.

"You, I'm sure, know everyone here in the village," Grey said quietly. "I want to know who the young woman is who goes about in a kerchief, wears a dress with a rose pattern, is dark and not very tall, from seventeen to twenty years of age. I met her not far from here. What is her name?"

The firm and precise way in which Grey questioned him forced Manners to reply in the same straightforward tone. He snickered a bit to himself, but remained obedient to the spirit in which he had been addressed. He could not resist pausing for a moment before he replied, in the vain hope of guessing what it was all about.

"Hmmm," he said, raising his eyes to the ceiling. "That must be 'Sailing Ship Asole.' It really couldn't be anyone else. She is a half-wit."

"Really?" said Grey, taking a gulp of rum.

And Hin told Grey how seven years before,

the little girl had talked with an itinerant collector of folk songs on the seashore. It must be admitted that since the day the beggar had set the story in circulation in this very tavern, it had been embroidered considerably. Its essence, however, had remained intact.

"And since that time they call her 'Sailing Ship Asole,'" Manners concluded.

Grey gazed mechanically at Letika, who sat as quietly and modestly as before, and then his eyes roamed out onto the dusty road in front of the tavern and he felt as if he had been hit at once in the heart and the head. Walking up the road, her face toward him, was that very same "Sailing Ship Asole" about whom Manners had just been speaking so clinically. Her features, illuminated by her wide-open eyes, had a simple but indelibly exciting quality. The seaman and Manners sat with their backs to the window, and to prevent them from turning by chance, Grey boldly shifted his glance to Hin's red eyes. All the disappointment of Manners' story was dissolved by the sight of Asole's eyes. Without suspecting a thing, Hin continued:

"I can also inform you that her father is a real scoundrel. He drowned my papa like a blind kitten, God forgive . . ."

He was interrupted by a wild roar from behind. The coalman, rolling his eyes, had suddenly emerged from the numbness of his hangover, and burst into song so violently that everyone was startled.

"Little basket, little basket,
Cheat us all with every basket! . . ."

"You've got a load on again, you damned old whaleboat!" shouted Manners. "Get out of here!"

"But just you fear
To land right here
In our Palestine!"

The coalman howled out his song and having finished, dipped his mustache into his splashing glass, as if nothing had happened.

Hin Manners shrugged his shoulders in anger. "Not a man—just garbage," he said solemnly. "Every time it's the same story!"

"Is there anything more you can tell me?" asked Grey.

"I've been telling you that her father is a scoundrel. Because of him, your grace, I was left an orphan, and as a mere child had to earn my subsistence. . . ." Manners said, moving back to the bar.

"You're a liar!" unexpectedly declared the coalman. "You've been lying so outrageously and hypocritically that it's made me sober."

Before Manners could open his mouth, the coalman turned to Grey. "He's a liar. So was his father—and his mother for that matter. That's the breed they are. You can be certain she's as healthy in the head as you and I. I've talked with her. She's sat on my cart eighty-four times or maybe a little less. When she was walking back from town and I had sold all my coal, I'd let her ride, of course. Why not? And I say she has a good head. One can see it right away. Of course she wouldn't say two words to Hin Manners. But I, dear sir, a freeman and a coal seller, despise loose talk and gossip. She talks like someone quite grown up, but her way of talking is a bit queer. You listen—and it's exactly what you and I might have said, but still not quite the same. In the village, for example, there was talk once about her trade. 'Here's what I'll tell you,' she said, and she held on to my shoulder like a fly to the belfry. 'My work is not boring, but I always want to think up something very special. I want to be so skillful that my toy boats will seem to float right there on my bench, and my oarsmen will look as if they are really rowing, and one knows that when they reach the shore and make fast, they will, as expected, go to get a bite.' I laughed so much over this. To me it was very funny. So I said to her, 'Well, Asole, you're that kind of person, and that's the reason you think the way you do. But look around you. People at work are like people fighting.' 'No,' she says. 'I know what I know. Whenever a fisherman goes fishing he thinks he will catch a bigger fish than anyone else has ever caught.' 'And what about me?' 'And you,' she laughs. 'You probably think when you fill up your twig basket with coal that it is just about to burst into flower.' Now that's exactly what she said! Right then and there I got the urge, I admit, to take a look into my empty coal basket. And all of a sudden it seemed to me as if the twigs sprouted buds and then burst into full leaf. Suddenly the vision disappeared. It even sobered me up a bit. And Hin Manners lies all over the place. I know him."

Since the conversation had become openly insulting, Manners glared at the coalman from behind the bar and inquired bitterly, "Do you want anything more?"

"No," said Grey, getting out his money. "We're leaving. Letika, you stay in town till evening and then come back to the ship. Find out whatever you can. And keep your mouth shut! Understand?"

"My most excellent captain," said Letika with a degree of familiarity he would not have used had it not come directly from the glass of rum, "only a deaf man could fail to understand that."

"Very good. Remember also that under no circumstances are you to talk about me or even mention my name."

Grey got up and went out. From that very

moment he was possessed by the presentiment of astonishing discoveries.

He could not manage to gather his thoughts together until he had seated himself in the ship's skiff. Laughing, he stretched out his hand, palm upwards, toward the burning sun, just as he had once done as a boy for Poldychoke in the wine cellar. Then he pushed off and began to row swiftly in the direction of his ship.

ON THE EVE

On the eve of that day, seven years after Egl, the wandering song collector, had told the little girl about a ship with scarlet sails, Asole returned home from one of her weekly visits to the toy store with a sad and worried face. She had brought back all the merchandise she had taken to town. She was so upset she was unable to speak for a time. Only when she saw from Longren's face that he was expecting something far worse than what had actually happened did she begin to tell her story. Standing by the window as she spoke, she drew on the glass with her finger and absent-mindedly looked out to sea.

The owner of the toy store had begun by opening his account book and showing how much they owed him. She had shuddered at the sight of a three-figure number. "This is what you've bought since December," he told her.

91

"And over here is how much you've sold." He pointed to a figure in two numbers.

"It was upsetting and unpleasant. He was rude and I could tell by his face that he was angry. I would gladly have run away, but I was too ashamed. 'This is no longer profitable for me, dear,' he continued. 'Foreign toys are the style now. All the shops are full of them. And no one wants to buy these toys.' That's what he said, and a lot more, but I've mixed it all up and forgotten. He must have felt sorry for me then, because he advised me to try to sell my toys at the Children's Bazaar and at Aladdin's Lamp."

Now that she had related the main part of her story, the girl turned her head and looked shyly at the old man. Longren sat there, his head hung down, gripping his fingers between his knees. Feeling her stare he raised his head and sighed. Overcoming her dejection, the girl ran to him, squeezed herself onto the seat beside him, and pushing her light hand beneath the leather sleeve of his jacket, she laughed and looked her father in the face from below, with forced animation.

"Oh, now, that's nothing at all. Just you listen to what happened then. I went on from there to a tremendous, terrifying store. There was a mob of people in it and I got pushed around. Finally I got through the crowd and went up to a dark man in glasses. What I said to him I really can't remember. At the end he laughed, messed about in my basket, looked at one or two things, and then wrapped them up again as they were, in their cloths, and gave them back to me."

Longren listened angrily. It was as if he were there in the store watching his daughter struck dumb among a crowd of rich people, at a counter piled high with luxurious merchandise. A neat man in glasses was condescendingly explaining to her that he would be ruined if he tried to sell the simple little toys which Longren made. Unconcernedly and adroitly he set out before her on the counter collapsible models of buildings and railway bridges, precise miniature automobiles, electrical sets, and airplanes. They all smelled of paint and of school. According to what he said, nowadays, children, in their games, only imitated what their elders did.

Asole had also visited Aladdin's Lamp and two other shops but had not sold any toys.

On finishing the story, she got dinner ready. After he had eaten and had a cup of strong coffee, Longren said: "Since we've failed we will have to look for something else. Maybe I should go to sea again—on the *Fitzroy* or perhaps the *Palermo*. Of course, the shopkeepers know their business," he continued, in a thoughtful vein, still thinking about the toys. "Nowadays children do not play—they study. They are all studying, studying, and they'll never begin to live. It's all true, and it's too bad, really too, too bad. Do you think you can get along without me for one trip? I don't see how I can leave you here all by yourself."

"Well, I can work too, on the same ship as you. Perhaps in the buffet."

"No!" Longren emphasized the word with a blow of his palm on the table. "So long as I am alive you will not enter service. Besides, there's time to think about our situation."

He fell into a sullen silence. Asole made a place for herself beside him on the stool. He saw out of the corners of his eyes, without even turning his head, that she was trying to comfort him, and he almost smiled. But had he smiled at that moment he would have frightened and disturbed the girl. She, repeating something to herself, stroked his tangled gray locks, and kissed his mustache. Stopping up his ears with her thin little fingers she murmured, "Now you can't hear me when I say I love you."

While she played up to him, Longren sat there with the puckered face of someone afraid to breathe in smoke, but when he heard her, he laughed deeply and loud.

"You're a darling," he said simply. He stroked her cheek and then went down to the beach to inspect his boat.

Asole stood for a time in the middle of the room, lost in thought, wavering between the desire to give in to quiet sadness and the necessity of getting her chores out of the way.

Later, after having washed the dishes, she checked their remaining provisions in the cupboard. She did not need to weigh or measure anything to see that they would soon be out of flour, no matter how much they stretched what they had, and the bottom of the sugar can was already visible. The packets of tea and coffee were almost empty. And there was no cooking oil. There was a bag of potatoes, the food she liked least. Then she washed the floor and sat down to stitch flounces on a skirt which she had remade from some old clothing. But remembering that some pieces of the material she needed lay behind the mirror, she went to get them—and caught a glimpse of her reflection.

This is what she saw: In the walnut frame of the room's bright emptiness stood a girl, not too tall, dressed in cheap white muslin decorated with roses. Over her shoulders lay a gray silk kerchief. Her somewhat childlike face with its light tan was mobile and expressive. Her beautiful eyes were too serious for her years. Her face, slightly asymmetrical, could move

96

one with the delicate purity of its features. Each hollow, each prominence could, of course, have found its duplicate in a multitude of feminine faces, but taken all together, their character was totally original.

The girl in the mirror smiled because she could not help it. Her smile was sad. It seemed to Asole as if she were looking at a stranger. She pressed her cheek to the glass, closed her eyes, and quietly stroked the mirror over her reflection. A swarm of vague and tender thoughts arose within her. She straightened up, laughed, sat down and began to do her sewing.

There were two girls within her, two Asoles, intermingled in remarkable and beautiful disorder. One of them was the daughter of the sailor, the craftsman, who carved toys. The other was a living lyric poem with all the miracles of a poem's harmonies and imagery, its secret juxtaposition of words in all their interplay of light and shadow. She knew life within the boundaries set for her by her experience, but over and above everyday matters, she had thoughts of a completely different order. Just as when we see objects we notice in them intuitively something more than their bare appearance, something human and different, so Asole saw beyond the visible. She was able to read and she loved reading, but even in a book she read principally between the lines. Everything merely comprehensible, not carried further by her own insights, was alien to her mind. Everything that she saw, that surrounded her, became a lacework of secrets which had only taken on the form, the image, of everyday life. The physical barriers of life collapsed, like stillness in the stroke of a bow against a violin string. More than once, excited and shy, she would go out at night to the seashore where, waiting for the dawn, she searched with great seriousness for the ship with the scarlet sails. These minutes were happiness to her. For most of us it is difficult to enter into a fairy tale. But for her it was just as hard not to believe in its power and enchantment.

At other times, thinking about all this, she was sincerely surprised at herself, not believing that she believed. Saying farewell to the sea with a smile and sadly coming back to reality, the girl smoothed the flounces of her dress and thought about her life. In it there was much that was boring and ordinary. Loneliness sometimes lay heavy on her heart. Within her there had already appeared that furrow of internal shyness, that martyr-like wrinkle, that prevented the giving and receiving of joy. The villagers said, "She's touched," "She's not there." She had become accustomed to this pain too. Sometimes she bore insults to the point where her breast ached just as if she had been physically struck. As a woman she was unpopular in Caperna. But many suspected, though in some vague and fantastic way, that she had been endowed with greater gifts than the others. The inhabitants of Caperna adored thick, heavy-set women with oily skin on their stocky calves and powerful hands. Here couples courted one another with hands groping down the back and nudging and pushing, as if they were at a bazaar. The most typical expression for such feelings was the frank simplicity of a roar.

Asole was as much at home among them as an easily frightened person would be among a group of ghosts. Had she possessed the charm of Aspasia, anything to do with love was unthinkable here. The beautiful sadness of a violin is powerless to change the direction of a regiment marching to the hooting of an army bugle. On all of this the girl had turned her back.

And while her head hummed with the song of life, her small hands worked effectively and skillfully. When she bit a thread, she looked into the distance, but this did not stop her from tucking in the hem smoothly or stitching the seam for a buttonhole with the accuracy of a sewing machine. Though Longren did not return, she was not worried about her father. Of late he would go out often to fish at night or simply to get a breath of fresh air.

She was not fearful. She knew that nothing bad would happen to them. In this respect Asole was still the same little girl who prayed in her own way, murmuring each morning with love, "Good morning, God!" And each evening, "Goodnight, God!"

In her opinion this brief acquaintanceship with God was quite sufficient to insure that He would keep unhappiness away from their door. She looked at it from His point of view. God was kept eternally busy with the affairs of millions of people. And therefore, in her opinion, one should accept the everyday shadows of life like the tactful guest who, when he visits a houseful of people, waits patiently for the busy host and in the meantime looks after himself as best he can.

When she finished her sewing, Asole put her work down on the corner table. She undressed and lay down to go to sleep. She had put out the lamp but soon realized that she was not sleepy. Her head was as clear as at midday. Even the darkness around her seemed artificial. Her body too, like her consciousness, was wide awake. Her heart was beating with the speed of a pocket watch. It was as if it were beating between the pillow and her ear. Asole grew angry, turning and twisting, first throwing off her blanket and then pulling it up to her chin. At long last she succeeded in raising in her mind's eye an image which usually helped her go to sleep. She imagined herself throwing stones into bright water and watched the ripples move out from them in circles. Sleep had been waiting for her help. It came, whispered back and forth with her dead mother, who stood at the head of the bed, and, obeying her smile, pronounced, "Sh, sh, sh." Asole slept immediately. She dreamt her favorite dream: flowering trees, longing, enchantment, songs, and secret things. But when she awoke, she remembered, with a cold chill, only the glitter of deep blue water rising from her feet to her heart. Having seen all this, she remained for a while longer in that impossible country and then awoke and sat up.

Sleep had fled as if she had not been asleep at all. A feeling of newness, gladness, and the desire to do something warmed her. She looked about her with that look with which one examines a new home. The dawn crept in—not in its full clarity but with that vague light in which one can begin to see one's surroundings. The bottoms of the windows were still dark, while up above, at the tops, they had grown light. Outside, almost at the very edge of a window frame, shone the morning star. Knowing she would not get back to sleep, Asole dressed, went to the window, undid the hook, and pushed it open. Outside lay expectant and clear-cut stillness. It was as if it had just that moment set in. In the dark blue shadows the bushes glistened. Farther away the trees slept. Everything breathed of closeness and of earth.

Holding on to the top part of the window frame, the girl looked out and smiled. Suddenly something like a distant call stirred within her, and it seemed as if she was awakening again out of one reality into another even more manifest. From that moment on a joyous awareness did not leave her. We hear and think we understand the speeches people make, and yet if what has been said is repeated, we often understand it in a different way. So it was with Asole.

She picked up her old kerchief, held it beneath her chin with her hand, locked the door, and rushed barefoot into the road. All was empty and quiet, yet it seemed to her that she was singing out like an orchestra and that everything could hear her. It was lovely and it gladdened her. The dark dust tickled her bare feet. She breathed brightly and happily. Against the open spaces of the heavens where the night still lingered, roofs and clouds stood out as darker shapes. The fences, sweetbriers, vegetable gardens, orchards, and the hardly visible road still drowsed. This seemed to be a different order of things than in the daytime. All was the same, but in shapes and relationships that normally escaped one. Everything was sleeping, but with open eyes which were secretly watching the girl.

The farther she went, the faster she walked, hastening to leave the village behind. Beyond Caperna stretched meadows. Beyond the meadows on the slopes of the hills along the shore grew hazelnut bushes, poplars, and chestnuts. Where the road came to an end and became a thickly overgrown path, a fluffy black dog with a white breast and anxious eyes turned and twisted at Asole's feet. The dog, recognizing Asole, whining and wagging his body, minced along at her side. Noticing his companion's smile, the dog grimaced gaily, wagged his tail, and ran ahead. Suddenly he sat down and with his paw vigorously scratched an ear. Then he ran back and away.

Asole went on into tall meadow grass which sprinkled her with dew. Holding her hands palms down over clusters of flowers, she moved on, smiling at their moist touch. Peeping into the special faces of the flowers, among the confusion of stalks, she distinguished nearly human traits—poses, movements, features, and glances. She would not have been surprised if at that moment there had appeared a procession of field mice, a parade of gophers, or if she had heard the crude merriment of a hedgehog who had just frightened a sleeping gnome with his snorting. And in fact a graying hedgehog rolled out in front of her on the pathway. "Huff, huff," he said intermittently with all his heart, like a coachman blustering at a pedestrian.

Asole spoke with the things she saw and understood them. "Hello, my sick one," she said to a purple iris which had been eaten full of holes by a worm. "You must stay at home!" she told a bush which was stranded in the middle of the path and whose leaves had been torn by the clothes of passersby. A big beetle had grabbed hold of a bluebell that was bending with his weight, and even though he was falling off, he stubbornly kept pushing at it with his legs. "Throw that fat passenger off!" Asole advised. The beetle, not able to hold his ground, flew off crackling. And thus, excited, elated, she approached the slope of the hill. Thickets still concealed an expanse of meadow, but now she was surrounded by her real friends. They were the great, ancient trees which grew among honeysuckle and hazelnut bushes. Their low hanging branches touched the top leaves of the bushes. In the large-leafed foliage of the chestnuts were white cones of flowers, where fragrance mingled with the smell of dew and of tar. The narrow path, sprinkled with slippery roots, sometimes descended and sometimes climbed the slope. Asole felt herself at home. She greeted the trees as people, touching them by their broad leaves. She went along whispering, at times to herself and at times out loud.

"Oh, here you are! And here is another you! There are so many of you, my little brothers! I am on my way. I am in a hurry. Let me through! I remember all of you and I love you." The "little brothers" stroked her majestically with their leaves. She made her way out of the grove, soiling her feet in the earth, to the cliff above the sea and stood at its edge out of breath from her rapid walk. A deep, invincible faith, triumphant, roared like the surf within her. The sea, outlined at the horizon by a golden thread, was still sleeping. Only beneath the bluff, in the puddles of shoreline pits, did the water rise and fall. The steely color of the sleeping ocean had turned dark blue and black near the shore. Beyond the golden thread the heavens, beginning to blaze, shone in an enormous fan of light. The white clouds were touched with a pale glow. Delicate pastel colors were reflected in them. In the black distance a trembling snowy whiteness had already appeared. The foam gleamed and the crimson sphere which rose to cut the golden thread cast a scarlet ripple across the width of the ocean, reaching right up to Asole's feet.

She sat down, hugging her knees to her chest. Leaning attentively toward the sea, she looked at the horizon with wide-open eyes in which there was nothing left of the adult. Everything for which she had waited for so long and so ardently was happening out there, at the edge of the world. In the distant depths she saw an underwater mountain from which climbing plants floated upwards. There were rounded leaves, pierced at the very surface by their stalks, and fantastic shining flowers. The highest leaves glistened above the water. Those who, unlike Asole, understood nothing at all would have seen only the shimmering and quivering of the ocean.

From among the rushes a sailing ship appeared. It sailed and stopped right in the middle of the dawn. At this distance it was clearly visible, like a cloud. Radiating joy, it glowed, like wine, like a rose, like blood, like lips, a scarlet velvet, a crimson fire. The ship sailed straight for Asole. Wings of foam quivered beneath the powerful weight of its keel. Standing, the girl pressed her arms to her breast as the wonderful play of light passed over into the after-swell. The sun rose and the bright fullness of the morning tore the cover from everything that had not yet come to life, from all that still hugged the sleepy earth.

The girl sighed and looked around. The music in her ears had ceased, but Asole was under its spell. The impression gradually weakened, becoming a memory which was finally transformed into simple fatigue. She lay down on the grass, yawned, and closed her eyes. She fell soundly asleep, snug as a walnut in its shell, without worry or dreams.

She was awakened by flies walking along

her bare foot. Turning it nervously, Asole opened her eyes. She sat up and started to pin up her disheveled hair. She felt something on her hand and at first thought it was a stalk caught between her fingers. Impatiently she raised her hand to her eyes and jumped to her feet with the force of a spurting fountain.

On her finger glittered the ring put there by Grey. For a moment she couldn't believe that it was her own finger. "Whose joke is this?" she cried out. "Am I still asleep? Could I have found it and forgotten?" She examined the ring with astonishment and glanced questioningly toward the sea and the surrounding greenery. But nothing even rustled; no one was hiding in the bushes, nor was there a sign of a boat on the dawn-lit sea. There was no explanation for what had happened, but without words or thoughts she understood. Trembling, she tore the ring off her finger, and held it cupped in her hand. She stared at it with all her heart, with all her soul, with all the mystic faith of youth, and then she hid it in her bodice. Asole covered her face in her hands and from behind them burst into a smile. Then, head down, she slowly made her way home.

Thus, by chance, but inevitably, Grey and Asole found each other on the morning of a summer day.

BATTLE PREPARATIONS

When Grey climbed up on the deck of *The Secret,* he stood for several minutes, stroking his head with his hand from back to front in a gesture of confusion, an absent-minded smile on his face. His mate, Panten, at this moment appeared on the quarter-deck with a plateful of fried fish. When he saw Grey he immediately noticed the captain's odd behavior.

"Are you hurt?" he asked cautiously. "Where have you been? Well, that, after all, is none of my business. There's an agent who's offering us profitable freight plus a bonus. What *is* wrong with you?"

"Thank you," said Grey, with a sigh of relief, like one who had just been freed. "The practical sound of your voice was just what I needed. It was like cold water. Panten, tell the men we are going to raise anchor today and move into the mouth of the Liliana, ten miles away. The channel is full of sandbars. We can enter it only from the sea. Come to my cabin and get the chart. We will not take on a pilot. For the time being, that is all. . . . Oh, yes— freight I need just as much as last year's snow. Tell that to the agent. I'm going off to town and won't be back till evening."

"What's happened?"

"Absolutely nothing, Panten. And for your own information, I don't want to be questioned. When the time comes, I'll tell you what it's all about. Simply tell the men we need repairs and that the local drydock is occupied."

"Very well," said Panten doubtfully to Grey's departing back. "Your orders will be carried out."

Though the captain's orders were fully intelligible, the mate, wide-eyed with surprise, dashed into his cabin, plate in hand, muttering, "Panten, there's a riddle for you. Maybe he wants to try smuggling? Are we going to run up the Jolly Roger?" And Panten embarked on the wildest speculations.

Grey went down to his cabin, got some money, and returned across the bay to Lisse, where he soon appeared in the town's shopping district. He was now acting with determination and calm, having worked out his plan to the smallest detail. Each movement, thought, action, warmed him with delight.

Grey visited three shops, intent on getting precisely what he wanted, having already seen in his mind's eye the exact color he desired. In the first two shops he was shown cheap silks in gaudy shades intended to satisfy primitive tastes. In the third he found samples of better quality. The shopkeeper bustled about, glad to bring out materials that had for long lain unsold. Grey was as serious as an anatomist. Patiently he went through bolt after bolt, set some aside, pushed others away, unwound and examined in daylight such a multitude of lengths of scarlet silk that the shop looked as if it were on fire. Over the toe of Grey's boot lay a wave of purple. His hands and face glowed with a rosy reflection. Playing with the folds of lightly resistant silk, he studied the various shades: red, pale and dark rose; thick bursts of cherry, orange, and dark chestnut tones; shades of all strengths and subtleties. But for a long time the captain could not find the true scarlet he sought. What the shopkeeper brought him was adequate, but none of it called forth that unequivocal "yes."

At last a silk was brought out that immediately attracted the customer. He sat down in an armchair at the window, pulled a long length from the noisy silk, tossed it across his legs, and sat back, pipe in his mouth, in motionless contemplation. A completely pure color, like a scarlet ray of morning, full of noble joy and royalty, it was exactly the proud color for which Grey had been searching. In it were no mingled shades of fire, poppy petals, no play of violet or lilac, no tinge of dark blue, nor any show of a tone that raised his doubt. It glowed like a smile. Grey became so lost in thought that he forgot the shopkeeper, who was waiting as tensely as a hunting dog at point. Tired of waiting, the tradesman reminded Grey of his presence by tearing off a piece of material.

"I've seen enough samples," said Grey, getting up. "I will take this silk."

"The whole piece?" the tradesman asked in a respectfully dubious voice. But Grey looked him silently in the forehead. The shopkeeper, becoming a little less polite, insisted, "How many yards, please?"

Grey motioned him to wait a moment, got out his pencil, and calculated what he needed.

"Two thousand yards," he said, inspecting the shelves doubtfully. "Yes, indeed, no more than two thousand yards."

"Two?" said the storekeeper, jumping convulsively like a spring. "Two thousand? Yards? I beg you to sit down, Captain. Wouldn't you care to look at samples of newer materials? Whatever you like. Here is some excellent tobacco. Here are some matches. Please! Two thousand, two thousand, at . . ." And he named a price which had as much relationship to the real price as an oath does to a simple "yes." But Grey was satisfied. He had no intention of haggling. "It's beautiful, the very best silk," continued the shopkeeper. "There's no better to be had anywhere. You can find it only here."

When at long last the merchant's praise had exhausted itself, Grey arranged for the delivery of the material, agreeing to pay the cost himself. He settled the bill and left, escorted to the door by a bowing, scraping storekeeper.

At that moment, across the street from the shop, an itinerant musician, having tuned up his cello, was making his strings speak out sadly and beautifully. His comrade, with a flute, added a throaty whistling to the singing of the cello. Grey heard the simple song which filled the hot, sleepy courtyard, and he knew immediately what he should do next. He made his way to the courtyard from which the music came. The tall flute player, with an appearance of downtrodden dignity was gratefully waving with his hat at those windows from which coins had been thrown. The cello had already been tucked beneath the arm of its owner who, wiping his perspiring forehead, was waiting for his comrade.

"Hello! Why, it's you, Zimmer!" Grey said to the cellist, recognizing him as the same person who entertained sailors with his fine fiddling at the Money on the Barrel Head Tavern. "How does it happen that you've given up the violin?"

"Most worthy captain," Zimmer explained with a self-satisfied expression. "I play everything that sounds and rattles. I was a musical clown once, when I was a lot younger. Now I have a yen for art, but I see, to my grief, that I've spoiled my unusual gift. Therefore out of belated pity for myself I have two loves—the cello and the violin. I play the cello in the daytime and the fiddle in the evenings. In other words, I weep and I sob over my lost talent. How about treating us to a bit of wine, eh? The cello, that's my Carmen, and the fiddle . . ."

"Is Asole," said Grey.

Zimmer misunderstood him.

"Yes," he nodded. "A solo on the cymbals or on brass trumpets—that's something very different. Anyway, what's it to me! Let the Pagliaccis take on airs. I know that magic exists in the violin and the cello."

"And what about my 'tur-lyur-lyu,'" demanded the flutist, a great big fellow with light blue sheep's eyes and a fair beard.

"It all depends on how much you drank in the morning. Sometimes there's a canary there and sometimes just wine fumes. Captain, this is my friend, Douce. I've already told him how you squander money when you drink, and he's loved you without ever even having seen you."

"Yes," said Douce. "I love generosity. But I'm shrewd. Don't believe my repulsive flattery."

"Listen," said Grey chuckling, "I have no time to waste and it's an urgent matter. I'll give you a chance to earn some good money. Get me an orchestra. But not one consisting of fancy dandies with the solemn faces of corpses who, in musical hairsplitting and gastronomy of sound, lose the soul of the music. Get me some of your own lads who can make the simple hearts of cooks and house servants weep. Gather your beggars together. The sea and love don't tolerate pedants. I would be delighted to sit down with you, and with more than one bottle in front of us, but I must go. There is a piece of business which I have to get out of the way. Take this and drink to the letter A. And if you agree to my proposal, come out to *The Secret* this evening. She's anchored not far from the breakwater at the head of the bay."

"Agreed!" shouted Zimmer, knowing that Grey paid like a king. "Douce, bow down, say Yes, and doff your hat. Captain Grey is getting married!"

"Yes," said Grey, simply. "I'll tell you all the details when you're aboard *The Secret*. You're . . ."

"To the letter A!" Douce winked at Grey, jostling Zimmer's elbow. "But—there are so many letters in the alphabet! How about something for Y?"

Grey handed over some more money. The musicians left. Then he went into a brokerage office and gave confidential instructions for a large sum to be delivered to him within six days. At the same time that Grey was returning to his own ship, the broker's representative was boarding an ocean steamer. By evening the silk had been delivered to *The Secret*. Five sailmakers, hired by Grey, had berthed in with the sailors. Letika had not yet returned, nor had the musicians arrived. While waiting for them, Grey went off to chat with Panten.

It should be noted that Grey had had the same crew for several years. At first the captain had surprised his sailors with his caprices, his unexpected journeys and stops—sometimes lasting for months—in the most unmercantile and unpopulated places. But gradually they had gotten used to the "Greyism" of Grey. He often sailed with ballast alone, having refused to take profitable freight, for the sole reason that he disliked the goods offered. No one could persuade him to carry soap, nails, machine parts, and other merchandise that lay in the murky silence of the hold, breathing forth an atmosphere of tedious necessity. On the other hand, he was always willing to load fruits, porcelain, livestock and other animals, spices, tea, tobacco, coffee, silk, and valuable species of trees such as sandalwood, ebony, and palm. All of these things satisfied his imagination and helped create a colorful atmosphere. It was not surprising that the crew of *The Secret*, having been indoctrinated in this spirit, looked somewhat condescendingly on other vessels which to them seemed enveloped in the fog of trivial gain. Nevertheless, this time Grey encountered questioning faces. Even the most stupid of his sailors knew that there was not the slightest need to carry out repairs in the mouth of a forest river.

Panten, of course, had reported Grey's orders. When Grey returned, his mate, smoking his sixth cigar, was pacing back and forth in the cabin, a bit groggy from the thick smoke and bumping into chairs. The evening had come. A golden beam penetrated through the ocean porthole and caught the shiny tip of the captain's service cap in its light.

"Everything is ready," said Panten gloomily. "If you wish, we can raise anchor."

"You ought to know me a bit better, Panten," Grey commented softly. "There is no mystery about what I'm doing. Just as soon as we drop anchor in the Liliana, I will tell you everything and then you won't have to waste so many matches on cheap cigars. Go ahead, lift anchor."

Panten, laughing awkwardly, scratched his brow.

"That's the way it is, of course," he said. "Anyway, as far as I'm concerned, it's all right."

When he departed, Grey sat for a while without moving, watching the half-opened door. Finally he went to his own cabin, where he alternately sat or lay down, listening to the creak of the windlass winding up the noisy chain. He started to go out to the forecastle but stopped midway and went back to his table, where in a gesture of thoughtfulness, he drew a line down its oilskin cloth with his finger. A blow of a fist on his door roused him from his trance. He turned the key and Letika came in. The sailor, breathing heavily, looked like a messenger who had arrived just in time to avoid being executed.

"'Fly fast, Letika,' I said to myself," he blurted out, "as soon as I saw from the cable pier how our lads were dancing around the windlass and spitting on their hands. I have eyes like an eagle. And I really flew. I breathed so hard down the boatman's neck that he was in a sweat from excitement. Captain—were you going to leave me stranded ashore?"

"Letika," said Grey, peering at his red eyes, "I was expecting you no later than this morning. Have you poured cold water on the back of your neck?"

"Yes—not so much as I took internally, but I poured some. Everything has been done as you asked."

"Tell me about it."

"No point in telling about it, Captain. I've written everything down right here. Take it and read it. I worked very hard at this. I'm going outside."

"Where?"

"I see by the reproach in your eyes that I'd better pour a lot more cold water on the back of my neck."

He turned and went out with the stumbling motions of a blind man. Grey unrolled the paper. Here is what Letika had written, in a scrawl that resembled a tumbledown fence:

"According to instruction! After five o'clock I walked along the street. A house with a gray roof with two windows on the side. A vegetable garden next to it. The designated female came out twice: for water, once, for kindling for the stove, second. When darkness came I strained my eyes to get a look into the window, but saw nothing because of a curtain."

There followed some notes on family matters which Letika had evidently collected from talk at the inn, since his memorandum concluded somewhat unexpectedly with the words: "On account of expenses I used a little bit of my own."

The essence of his report added nothing, however, to what we already know. Grey put the paper into his desk, whistled for the officer of the watch, and sent for Panten. But the boatswain, Atwood, put in an appearance instead, pulling at his rolled-up sleeves.

"We've cast off at the breakwater," he said. "Panten sent me to find out what you want. He's busy because some people with drums, fiddles, and horns are arguing with him. Did you invite them aboard *The Secret?* Panten wants you to come and speak to them. His head is spinning."

"Yes, Atwood," said Grey. "I did invite the musicians aboard. Tell them to go to the crew's quarters for now. We'll see later on where to put them up. And, Atwood, tell them and the crew that I'll be on deck in fifteen minutes. Get them together. You and Panten be there too."

Atwood, raising his left brow, sidled out of the door. Grey spent ten minutes with his hands over his face, gathering his thoughts. Meanwhile, all on the ship awaited him, full of curiosity and impatient conjecture. When he appeared, he saw in their faces the expectation of something fantastic. Since to him what was taking place seemed quite natural, he felt a slight disappointment in the tension of the others.

"There is nothing special," Grey said, seating himself on the companionway bridge. "We will remain here in the mouth of the river until we have changed all our rigging. You have seen that red silk has been shipped aboard. From it, under the direction of master sailmaker Blant, new sails are to be made for *The Secret*. Then we will sail—where, I will not yet say. In any case, it won't be far. I am going to my wife. That is, she is not yet my wife, but she will be. I need scarlet sails so that she will see me from afar, as has been promised her. You can see there's no mystery here. That will be all."

"Yes," said Atwood, seeing from the smiling faces of the sailors that they were pleasantly puzzled, yet too shy to ask questions. "So that's what it's all about, Captain. Not our place to judge such matters. As you want it, that's the way it'll be. I congratulate you."

"Thank you."

Grey pressed the hand of the boatswain, who in turn pressed the captain's with such strength that he gave in. Then all the rest of the crew came up, one after another, with shy warmth in their eyes and muttered congratulations. No one shouted or was unruly. The sailors had seen something not entirely ordinary in the words of the captain. Panten sighed with relief and Grey became gayer, the weight on his soul having lifted. Only one of the ship's carpenters seemed dissatisfied with something. Offering a fishlike hand to Grey, he asked gloomily, "What gave you that idea, Captain?"

"It came to me like a blow from your hatchet," Grey replied. "Zimmer! Bring your lads over here."

The fiddler, whacking his musicians on the back, pushed and pulled out of the crowd eight sloppily dressed men.

"This one here, he's the trombone," said Zimmer. "He doesn't play—he booms like a cannon. These two boys who don't shave yet are the bugles. You hear them and you want to fight right away. Then comes the clarinet, the cornet, and the second violin. They are all great experts at crowding the lively first violin. In other words, me. And here is the chief boss of our jolly trade—the drummer, Fritz. Drummers usually have, as you know, a disappointed look, but this one beats his drums with dignity and concentration. In his playing there is something open and direct, like his drumsticks. Is everything to your liking, Captain Grey?"

"Excellent," said Grey. "You've all been provided with hammocks in the hold, which for this trip has been loaded with various 'scherzos,' 'adagios,' and 'fortissimos.' Panten, loose the moorings. Let's get going! I'll take over from you in two hours' time."

The two hours passed without his noticing them, for he was in the company of that inner music which had become as much a part of his consciousness as the pulse is of the arteries. He thought about one thing, wanted one thing, strove toward one thing. A man of action, in his thoughts he jumped the course of events, regretting only that he could not move as quickly as in a game of checkers. Nothing in his calm exterior revealed the tension of his feelings, which, like an enormous bell clanging above his head, resounded through his entire being. To calm himself he began to count: "One . . . two . . . thirty . . ." And so forth, until he reached "a thousand." This worked. He was capable, at last, of looking at the whole enterprise from the sideline. What surprised him was that he could not picture the inner Asole since he had never even spoken to her. He had read somewhere that it was possible, to some small extent, to understand a person by imagining his face and imitating its expression. Grey's eyes soon began to assume a strange untypical look and his lips began to form themselves into a weak and gentle smile, when suddenly he burst out laughing and went out to relieve Panten.

It was dark. Panten, with the collar of his jacket raised, was pacing back and forth at the compass, directing the helmsman: "Port one quarter point, port. Stop. A quarter point more." *The Secret* was sailing half-rigged before a tailwind.

"You know, Grey," said Panten, "I'm satisfied."

"With what?"

"With exactly what you are satisfied with. I've now understood everything. Right here on the bridge." He winked slyly, lighting up his smile with the embers in his pipe.

"Well," said Grey, suddenly guessing what Panten meant. "What is it that you've understood?"

"It's the best way of smuggling," Panten whispered. "Anyone can use any color sails he pleases. You are a genius, Grey!"

"Poor Panten!" said the captain, not knowing whether to be angry or to laugh. "Your guess is very clever, but there's nothing to it. Go along and sleep. I give you my word that you are mistaken. I am doing exactly what I said I was doing."

He checked the ship's course and sent the mate off to sleep.

Longren spent the night at sea. He did not sleep nor did he fish. Instead he sailed aimlessly, listening to the splashing of the water, gazing into the darkness, letting himself be caressed by the wind and immersed in thought. In the worst hours of life there was nothing that could restore his peace of mind as could these lonely wanderings. Stillness, just stillness, and no people nearby, was what he needed in order to hear and understand the distant, confused voices of his inner world. This night he thought about the future, about poverty, about Asole. It was extremely difficult to leave her even for a short time. He also feared to reawaken that pain within himself that had been stilled. Perhaps when he embarked on a ship again, he would imagine that back there in Caperna his wife had never died and was waiting for him. But returning, he would approach his home knowing that Mary would never again run from the threshold to meet him. Yet Asole must have food, and he decided to act as his concern for her directed.

When Longren returned home, Asole was still not back. Her early walks did not as a rule make her father anxious. This time, however, there was a touch of nervousness in his waiting. Pacing from corner to corner, on one of his turns he suddenly saw her. She had entered impetuously and stood without speaking in front of him, nearly frightening him with the bright light of her gaze. It seemed as if she had revealed her second face—that true face of a human being that usually exists only in the eyes. She said nothing and stared at Longren with such an incomprehensible look that he quickly asked, "Are you ill?"

She did not reply at once. When the question finally got through to her, Asole trembled like a branch which had just been pushed back and let go. "No, I am well. . . . Why are you looking at me that way? I am just happy. I'm not happy because this is such a good day. But what have you got on your mind? I can see by your face that you have some plan or other."

"No matter what I might think up," said Longren, seating the girl next to him, "I know you will understand. We have nothing to live on. I don't want to ship out as a seaman on long cruises, so instead I'm going to enter service on the postal steamer which travels between Lisse and Cassette."

"Yes," she said from far away, but making an effort to enter into his concern and his plan, knowing she was powerless to suppress her own gladness, "that's very unpleasant. I'll be lonely. Come back as soon as you can." After saying this, she broke into an irrepressible smile. "Yes, please come back quickly. I'll wait for you."

"Asole," said Longren, taking her cheeks in his hands and turning her toward him. "You must tell me what happened."

She felt that she must allay his alarm and compelled herself to be serious. It was only in her eyes that her new life did not cease to shine.

"You are strange," she said. "There was absolutely nothing. I was out gathering walnuts."

Longren wouldn't quite have believed this had he not been so taken up with his own thoughts. Their conversation became practical. He told her to pack his bag and enumerated all the things he needed to take.

"I'll be back in ten days' time," he said. "You are to pledge my gun at the pawn shop and stay here at home. If anyone tries to bother you, tell them Longren will be back soon. Don't worry about me. Nothing bad will happen to me."

After this he ate, gave his daughter a tender kiss, and tossing his bag over his shoulder, set out on the road to town. Asole watched him disappear until he was lost from view behind the turn and then went back to the house. She had much housework to do, but she had forgotten all about it. She looked around with an air of slight surprise, as if she no longer belonged to the house that had been etched in her consciousness since childhood. Now it looked to her as dear places look when one returns to them from a completely different way of life after a number of long years. There seemed to her to be something unworthy in this rebuff to her own home, something not quite right. She sat down at the table at which Longren carved his toys and tried to glue a wheel to the stern. Looking at these objects, she involuntarily saw them lifesize and real. Everything that had happened to her that morning, the golden ring, the mirrored sun that had fallen from across the sea at her feet, once again made her quiver with excitement.

She didn't sit still for long but left the house and went off on foot to Lisse. There was absolutely nothing that she needed to do there. She didn't even know why she went. She felt a compulsion to which she had to give in. On the way she met a pedestrian who asked for some directions. She explained to him clearly what he wanted to know and at once forgot all about him.

She noticed nothing along the way, as when she carried a hen which required all her attention. In Lisse she was entertained somewhat by the noises coming at her from all directions. The town no longer had the same effect on her as it once had, when frightening and overwhelming her, it had turned her into a speechless little coward. She walked slowly around the ring-shaped boulevard which cut through the dark blue shadows of trees. She gazed confidently and easily at the faces of passersby, moving at an even, self-assured pace. Observant persons noticed more than once that day the unknown girl, a bit odd in looks, who moved through the bright crowd with an air of deep meditation. In the square she put her hand in a fountain, deflecting the spray, and sat down to rest before returning to the forest road. She made her way home with a fresh heart, in a mood as clear and peaceful as an evening stream which has finally exchanged the many-hued reflections of the day for the even tone of twilight. Nearing the village, she met that same coalman who had once thought his basket was bursting into bloom. He stood near his cart with two strange, gloomy men who were covered with soot and mud. Asole was pleased to see him.

"Hello, Philip," she said. "What are you doing here?"

"Nothing, my little fly. My wheel came off. I fixed it. And now I'm chattering away with our boys. Where are you coming from?"

Asole didn't reply. Instead she blurted out, "You know, Philip, I like you very much and so I'm going to tell you something, just you. I am going away soon. Probably I'll be leaving here for good. Don't you tell anyone."

"You want to go away? Where are you planning on going? The astonished coalman opened his mouth questioningly, making his beard seem longer.

"I don't know," she said, studying the small clearing beneath the elm where the cart stood and the green grass in the rosy light of the evening and the black and silent coalman. Then, thoughtfully, she added, "I know neither the day nor the hour, and I don't even know where. I am not going to tell anyone else. Therefore, just in case, goodbye. You've given me many a lift."

She took his enormous black hand and shook it. The coalman's face cracked into a smile. The girl waved, turned, and went on. She disappeared so swiftly that Philip and his friends didn't even have a chance to turn their heads.

"Wonders!" said the coalman. "Just try to understand her. Something's going on with her today . . ."

"True," the second supported him. "She's talking strangely, saying queer things. Not our business."

"Not our business," repeated the third.

Then all three of them climbed into the cart, which went creaking off down the stony road and disappeared in the dust.

It was a bright morning hour. A light fog, full of strange visions, hovered over the immense forest. A hunter who had just left the warmth of his fire was moving slowly in the downstream direction of the river. Shafts of light came through the trees from its open expanse. But the eager hunter did not go down to the river itself. He was studying the fresh track of a bear which led to the mountains.

A sudden sound penetrated the woods. It was a clarinet singing out. One of Grey's musicians had gone out on deck and was playing a sad and repetitious melody. The sound trembled like a voice trying to conceal its grief. It rose, hesitated on a nostalgic note, and broke off. A distant echo vaguely repeated the tune.

The hunter, noticing a broken branch, followed the direction it indicated and pushed his way to the water. The fog had still not lifted.

It screened from view the outlines of an enormous sailing ship, slowly turning toward the mouth of the river. Its furled sails came alive, hanging festoonlike, straightening out and covering the masts with enormous impotent folds. Voices and steps were heard. The offshore wind lazily plucked at the sails. At last the sun's warmth produced the desired effect. A wind began to blow, dispersed the fog, and swept over the yardarms, billowing the sails into airy scarlet shapes. Rosy hues rippled along the whiteness of the masts and rigging. All was white except for the spread, evenly advancing sails, the color of profound gladness.

The hunter, watching from the shore, kept rubbing his eyes until he convinced himself that he was seeing exactly what he thought he was seeing. The ship disappeared behind a bend in the river, but he continued standing there. At last, shrugging his shoulders, he went on after his bear.

As *The Secret* moved down the river channel, Grey, afraid of sandbars, kept the wheel himself, and the helmsman stood by. The mate,

Panten, sat next to him in a new wool suit and a shiny new service cap. He was clean-shaven and meekly sulky. He still could not see the connection between the scarlet sails and Grey's avowed purpose.

"Now," said Grey, "with my sails glowing, and a fair wind, and more happiness in my heart than an elephant has when he sees a peanut, I am going to try to explain, as I promised you I would back in Lisse. Please understand I don't consider you stupid or stubborn. No, you are a model sailor and that is worth much. But like most people, you hear the voices of simple truths muffled by the thick window glass of life. They cry out to you, but you do not hear them. I believe that the ancient concept of the beautiful—the unattainable—is, in essence, just as attainable and possible as a walk in the country. Soon you will see a girl who cannot, and who must not, marry except precisely in the way which is being unfolded right in front of your eyes."

He told the sailor briefly the story that we already know, and in conclusion added: "You see how closely fate, will, and character are interwoven here. I have come to the person who is waiting only for me. I want only her, perhaps for the precise reason that thanks to her I have been able to understand one simple truth, that so-called miracles are made with one's own hands. When the most important thing for a man is to get a precious sixpence, it's easy enough to provide him with that sixpence. But when a heart conceals the seed of a flaming plant, a miracle, that is the miracle to make happen—if one can.

"The one you do it for will be reborn and so will you. When the chief warden himself frees a prisoner; when a billionaire presents a villa, a chorus girl, and a safe full of money to a clerk; and when a jockey just for once holds his horse back for the sake of a horse who's had a run of bad luck, everyone understands. That is nice, that is inexpressibly miraculous. But there are other miracles: a smile, gladness, forgiveness, and a word which is needed and said in time. To experience them is to possess everything. As for Asole and me, we will remain forever in the glow of scarlet sails created in the depths of a heart that knows what love is. Do you understand me?"

"Yes, Captain," Panten muttered, wiping off his mustache with a clean, neatly folded handkerchief. "I've understood everything. I am going below to ask Nick's forgiveness for scolding him yesterday for dropping a pail overboard. And I'll give him a bit of tobacco. He lost his at cards."

Before Grey, somewhat surprised at such a speedy reaction to his speech, could say anything, the mate crashed down the companionway and could be heard sighing in the distance. Grey looked around and then peered upwards. Silently the scarlet sails were moving ahead. The sunlight turned their seams a smoky purple. *The Secret* was running swiftly out to sea and leaving the shore behind. There were no doubts in Grey's mind, no dull pounding of alarm, no noise of petty concerns. As calm as one of his sails, he rushed toward his goal, filled with thoughts that flew faster than words.

At mid-morning the smoke of a navy cruiser

showed on the horizon. The cruiser changed course and from half a mile away raised its signal flag: "Lay to."

"Brothers," said Grey to the sailors, "we'll not be fired upon, have no fear. They simply can't believe their eyes."

He gave orders for his ship to lay to. Panten, shouting as if he were at a fire, brought the ship out of the wind. It came to a standstill. Meanwhile a steam launch with a crew and a lieutenant in white gloves was on its way from the cruiser. The lieutenant, climbing up on the deck of *The Secret*, looked about in amazement and followed Grey to his cabin. He emerged an hour later, and motoring back to his dark blue cruiser, he turned to wave at the captain, smiling as if he had received a promotion. Evidently this time Grey had had more success than with the simple-minded Panten. The cruiser, slowing down, fired a powerful salute into the horizon. The belching gunsmoke, driving through the air in enormous spheres, scattered in tufts above the quiet water. For the rest of the day there reigned on

146

the cruiser a sort of semi-holiday stupefaction, a mood which was out of step, unmilitary. From the bridge to the engine room everyone seemed to be under the influence of the banner of love. In the torpedo section the officer of the watch asked a passing sailor, "Tom, how did you get married?"

"I caught her by the skirt when she wanted to jump out of the window to get away from me," said Tom, as he proudly twisted his mustache.

For a time *The Secret* sailed on the open sea. By midday a distant shore appeared on the horizon. Taking his spyglass, Grey focused it on Caperna. Had it not been for a row of rooftops he could have seen Asole sitting at a window, reading. Along the page of her book there climbed a greenish little beetle. It stopped now and then, and rising on its front legs, it looked very independent and tame. It had already twice been blown off onto the window sill from which each time it had returned, trustingly and freely, as if it wanted to tell her something. This time it succeeded in almost reaching the girl's hand which held the corner of the page, but it got stuck on the word "look." Here it stopped in doubt, expecting a new squall. And, in actual fact, it just barely avoided trouble, since Asole had already exclaimed, "You're here again, you little beetle. Fool!" And she was about to blow her guest off into the grass, when suddenly her gaze, wandering from one rooftop to another, discovered a gap between them, revealing a distant patch of dark blue sea and a white ship with scarlet sails.

She trembled, leaned back as if frozen. Then she jumped up, her heart sinking, and burst into irrepressible tears. *The Secret* by this time had rounded a small promontory and was holding to shore on the port side. Soft music poured out into the sky-blue day from the white deck beneath the flame of scarlet silk. It was the rhythmic music of the familar: "Fill, fill the flowing cups, and drink, my friends, to love . . ." Its simple melody expressed rejoicing and excitement.

Not remembering how she had left the house, Asole ran toward the sea. At the first corner she stopped, almost too weak to go on. Her legs seemed like putty. Afraid she might faint, she stamped her feet and recovered her balance. At times the scarlet sails were hidden by a rooftop or a fence, and fearing they would disappear completely like a mirage, she hastened on, and only when she again saw the ship did she stop to catch her breath.

By this time there was such confusion, such excitement, in Caperna that even an earthquake could have no greater impact. Never before had a big sailing ship come to this coast. And the ship had those very scarlet sails that had been the subject of the villagers' ridicule. At this very moment these same scarlet sails were clearly and incontrovertibly moving into the harbor, innocently defying all the laws of sense. Men, women, and children rushed to the shore in whatever clothes they were in. They called to each other from house to house, argued, collided with each other, fell. Soon a crowd formed at the water's edge. Into this mob Asole ran headlong.

Before she arrived, her name was bandied

about by the malicious, grim, and nervous crowd. Mostly it was the men who spoke aloud. The stunned women sobbed in low tones with a snakelike hissing. When Asole appeared, everyone fell silent and made way for her in awe. She stood alone in the emptiness of the burning sand, embarrassed, shy, happy, with her face no less scarlet than the sails of her own miracle, helplessly reaching out her arms to the tall ship.

A skiff full of sunburned oarsmen left the ship and moved toward the shore. Among them stood erect that person whom, it seemed to her now, she had known and vaguely remembered from her childhood. He looked at her with a smile which warmed her and urged her on. And Asole, forgetting her fears, mistakes, mis-understandings, unknown obstacles, ran out up to her waist into the warm cradle of the waves.

Zimmer waved his baton and the familiar melody burst forth, but this time in a full, triumphant chorus. From excitement, from the movement of the clouds and the waves, the glitter of the water, the girl could no longer distinguish what was moving—she, the ship, or the skiff. Everything was in motion, whirling and subsiding.

But an oar splashed near her. She lifted her head. Grey bent down and she grasped him by the waist. She blinked, opened her eyes, and smiling, breathless, exclaimed, "You're just as I hoped!"

"And so are you, my little one!" cried Grey, pulling his Asole out of the water. "You see, I have come. Did you recognize me?"

She nodded. She held onto his waist, still blinking and trembling. When Asole at last could look about her, the rocking skiff, the glistening waves, the powerful approaching side of *The Secret*, seemed like a dream in which light and water played a game of reflections on a wall streaming with sunbeams. Held in Grey's strong arms, she climbed up the ship's ladder. The deck, covered with oriental rugs, basking in the scarlet splashes of the sails, was like a garden in paradise. And soon Asole was standing in Grey's cabin.

From above, the music swelled again. Once

more Asole closed her eyes, fearing that if she kept them open everything would disappear. Grey took her arms, and knowing now where she could find safety, she hid her face, wet with tears, on his chest. Carefully, but with a smile, shaken himself by the fact that the precious moment had arrived, Grey raised the long-dreamed-of face to his. In the girl's eyes he saw reflected everything that is best in a human being.

"Will you take my Longren too?" she asked.

"Yes." And he kissed her so hard in the wake of his iron "yes" that she laughed.

There are many words in the world, in many languages, but all of them together could not communicate what these two had to say to each other that day.

On the main deck, at the mainmast, the entire crew had gathered. And in their midst stood the old worm-eaten barrel with the top knocked out, revealing the ancient dark bliss it contained. Atwood stood. Panten sat importantly, glowing like a newborn babe. Grey came up on deck, signaled the orchestra, and the trumpets sang out. Removing his service cap, he was the first to fill his cutglass beaker with the ancient wine.

"There you are," he said, drinking down the wine and tossing away the glass. "Drink now, everyone drink! Whoever fails to drink is my enemy."

He did not need to repeat his words. While *The Secret*, at full speed ahead, raced away from awestruck Caperna, the crush around the barrel exceeded anything that had ever been seen even on the greatest of holidays.

"How did you like it?" Grey asked Letika.

"Captain!" said the sailor, searching for words. "I don't know whether it liked me, but I must consider carefully my impressions. Honey and a garden!"

"What?"

"I want to say that I feel as if a hive of honey and a garden have been stuffed into my mouth! Here's happiness to you, Captain. And happiness also to the one who, I must say, is the best 'freight' ever carried by *The Secret*, the best 'prize' of the ship."

When dawn broke the following day, *The Secret* was far from Caperna. Some of the crew were still lying on the deck, as they had collapsed in sleep, overcome by Grey's wine. Only the officer of the watch and the helmsman had remained on their feet. And a thoughtful, hung-over Zimmer was sitting in the stern with the fingerboard of the cello at his neck. He sat there quietly drawing his bow across the strings, making them speak in a magic and unearthly voice. And he thought about happiness.